GUARDING SALVATION

SHADOW ELITE BOOK ONE

MADDIE WADE

Guarding Salvation
Shadow Elite Book One
By Maddie Wade

Published by Maddie Wade

Cover: Clem Parsons-Metatec
Editing: Black Opal Editing
Formatting: Black Opal Editing

Acknowledgments

I am so lucky to have such an amazing team around me without which I could never bring my books to life. I am so grateful to have you in my life, you are more than friends you are so essential to my life.

My wonderful beta team, Greta, and Deanna who are brutally honest and beautifully kind. If it is rubbish you tell me, it is and if you love it you are effusive. Your support means so much o me.

My editing team—Linda and Dee at Black Opal Editing. Linda is so patient, she is so much more than an editor, she is a teacher and friend.

Thank you to my group Maddie's Minxes, your support and love for Fortis, Eidolon, Ryoshi, and all the books I write is so important to me. Special thanks to Rowena, Tracey, Faith, Rachel, Carolyn, Kellie, Maria, Greta, Deanna, Sharon, Becky, Vicky, and Linda L for making the group such a friendly place to be.

My ARC Team for not keeping me on edge too long while I wait for feedback.

Lastly and most importantly thank you to my readers who have embraced my books so wholeheartedly and shown a love for the stories in my head. To hear you say that you see my characters as family makes me so humble and proud. I hope you enjoy Bram and Aoife's story as much as I did.

Cover: Clem Parsons-Metatec
Editing: Black Opal Editing

AUTHORS NOTE

To make it easier for those of you who are unfamiliar with Irish names, Aoife is pronounced EE-fa and means "beautiful, radiant, joyful.".

PROLOGUE

His face hit the concrete stone of the wall as the copper threw him into the small cell. Anger and booze stopped the pain from the cut on his cheek from registering, the fury pounding through his blood the only thing he could think about as it consumed him.

"Quit yer blethering and sober up, lad. You'll be in front of a judge in the morning and he won't want to smell the fumes coming off ye and no be thinking a title is gonna save ya."

Bram ignored the desk sergeant as he closed the heavy metal door and locked him inside the six-by-six cell. Sounds of fighting and yelling came through from the surrounding cells, souls as lost as he was in this moment, and he wondered how his life had ended up here. Sitting on the small, hard bench that doubled as a bed, he rested his elbows on his knees and held his head. How had tonight gone so wrong? Nausea roiled in his belly like coiling snakes as the ale and shots of tequila began to wear off, the reality of his situation becoming clearer by the second.

He should be home in his luxury bed with a warm, willing body beside him. Instead, he was in a police holding cell waiting to see if a judge would grant him bail. The night had started well; he'd been in

1

the pub with his friends, chatting up some bird who was making it very clear she'd let him fuck her, when his younger sister had come in with her friends. Furious she was cockblocking him, he'd gone over and told her to go home or to move on to another pub, but Lana was eighteen, just a year younger than he was and could legally be there.

They'd argued and she'd left with her friends. He'd been happy he could relax with his mates and have some fun without worrying about her. No boy of nineteen wanted his younger sister cramping his style, especially one with the responsibilities he carried on his shoulders. He needed to just let loose and blow off some steam, forget who he was and what was expected of him for the night.

His arm around the girl, whose name he couldn't remember, he was about to ask her if she wanted to get some air, which they both knew was code for a quick fuck. Getting laid was easy for him, with ice-blue eyes, dark blond hair which sometimes looked auburn, two full sleeves of tattoos, and a six-pack that came from days on the estate doing physical labour, he knew he'd get his way. She was a sure thing, fucking the heir to a title was like a trophy to these girls. He didn't care, he wasn't going to marry them, just have some fun. His fifth pint had been sliding down easy when one of Lana's friends had come running into the pub.

Instantly his instincts had him moving toward the door and it got a little fuzzy after that, but he'd never forget seeing Lana on the ground in a disgusting alley not a street away, her lip split, her eye swollen, and her clothes ripped. One look into her dead-looking eyes and he'd known what had happened. Rage seared his blood, a fury so deep he could hardly breathe past it broke through as he bellowed his anger. Seeing the fear on his sister's face, he fought to rein in his rage.

"Who?" It was all he needed to know, revenge pumping through his blood and the desperate desire to kill the person who'd hurt her. He'd crouched beside her as her friends gathered around her. "Lana, please, tell me who did this." He softened his voice as she looked at him and a sob escaped her as she uttered his name.

"Ray Walsh."

"He's gonna pay, Lana."

"Bram, no!"

Bram had ignored her cries. That fucking bastard had been sniffing around Lana for months. Bram had thought his warning was enough and now this had happened. The slithering prick had violated his sister. He'd found Ray laughing in the pub, bragging about what he'd done in front of all his mates. He'd dragged him outside by his hair as he'd tried to get away and beaten him unconscious. It felt like a red mist had fallen over him; he was no longer himself, but a machine with only one thought and that was revenge. Over and over, he pummelled his fists into Walsh's face, seeing the blood splatter as bone and cartilage gave way under the force of his blows. Walsh had gone from a confident prick to the snivelling rat he was in moments as he saw the hatred in Bram's eyes and knew he'd get no redemption for his crimes.

Even as Walsh went from begging and crying to silent, he kept going. The rage, unlike anything he'd known before, completely taking over him. All he could see was the broken defeat on his sister's face.

He would've kept going but his friends pulled him away as the cops arrived. He remembered coming out of the fog of frenzied violence and seeing the blood dripping from his cracked knuckles. He should have felt bad but as the memories came back to him, Bram felt not an ounce of regret for what he'd done or that Walsh would be eating through a tube for months. No, his guilt lay with allowing it to happen in the first place.

If he'd just thought as a brother and not as some scrotum who only cared about getting his dick wet, then this wouldn't have happened. When they'd arrested him, he'd refused a lawyer, or any counsel, not wanting to drag his family name through the mud. His only call had been to his father to make sure Lana was okay.

He'd been relieved to hear she was, but furious that she wouldn't press charges and report her attack. He knew his father was probably behind that, the family name was important after all. He'd had it drilled into him since the day he was born that he was a McCullum and, as the son of Laird John McCullum, the twelfth Laird to own the title and the McCullum estate and castle, it was his duty to bring pride and never shame.

Bram did feel shame though for letting his sister get hurt in the first place. He'd failed her and now she'd live with the consequences of that for the rest of her life. All he'd ever wanted to do was live his life and make his family proud, to be worthy of the name McCullum. His father had sounded so shocked by his actions, so disappointed in him and what he'd done. He'd never wanted to bring dishonour to his family.

Now he'd done just that, and he knew he'd do it again if the choice was offered. He only wished he'd done it before that fecking shitehole touched his sister.

Lying back on the bench, he looked up at the ceiling of the cell, wishing he could go back in time and stop what had happened. Ray Walsh had always hated him. The Walsh family had some beef with his dad that he didn't understand nor care about. He wanted no part in the politics that came with owning the wealth and title he'd one day inherit. All he wanted was to finish his degree in Agricultural Economics and Business so he could make the estate thrive again.

He must have dozed off because he woke to the door being pulled open. He jumped to his feet, his head pounding and his gut churning. He paused to get his balance and flexed his fingers, which were torn and bloody, reminding him of what had happened a few hours earlier. The police station was eerily quiet now, with people sleeping off their drunken fights or coming to the realisation of what they'd done.

"You have a visitor."

"What time is it?"

"Five-thirty. Now get movin', I ain't your damn secretary."

Bram followed the copper, the same one who'd nicked him, down the corridor to the same interview room they'd used a few hours earlier. Inverness was a busy police station, especially on a Saturday night and he could hear the shouts and scuffles coming from near the desk where he'd been brought in earlier. It seemed only the cells were quiet, but the night was far from over for some.

He stepped into the room and was directed to a chair before the policeman left. Bram looked around, taking everything in and cataloguing the cameras, the exits, the threats before his eyes landed on the two-way mirror. He felt the hair prick up on the back of his neck like he was being watched. He didn't look away but continued to stare at whoever was watching him.

He had nothing to hide. Fuck, he'd confessed to everything, not arguing a single charge. The detective who'd charged him had even said he understood why he'd done what he did, and he was sorry that he'd now face a future with a record because of it. Of course, that had been off the record and would have no bearing on his sentence. He didn't care. Lana would have the biggest burden to carry, and it was his fault. He'd happily give up his life if it meant she didn't have to go through what she had.

The door opened and a man he'd never seen stepped into the room. He was tall, with dark hair and blue eyes, and looked like he wrestled tigers for a hobby. Everything about him screamed military, from his hair to the way he walked.

He sat down opposite Bram without a word and rested his arms on the desk in a relaxed manner. "I'm here to make you an offer."

Bram sat back, feeling more uncomfortable than he'd like to admit. This guy seemed cool, but everything about Bram was telling him he was a predator or could be if someone got on the wrong side of him. "Not interested."

The stranger grinned. It wasn't so much as friendly but more that he'd expected his response. "Come on now, Bram, you can do better than that. I know what you did, and I know why."

"I don't regret it. He fucking deserved more than I gave him."

"Agreed."

Bram was taken aback by this man's attitude. He'd been expecting a lecture on his behaviour and having more control. "What, no lecture on my lack of control?" Bram folded his arms in defence, trying to act like he wasn't intimidated by this bloke.

"Oh, your control definitely needs work. It needs to be channelled correctly. All that lethal, raw aggression needs to be honed and moulded. I can give you that. I can give you purpose and a future other than the one facing you now."

Bram shrugged. "It's an assault charge. I don't have a previous record. Worst I'll get is a few years in the slammer. I don't need a reference to inherit my title."

The guy smirked. "Except it isn't going to be an assault charge. Ray Walsh died twenty minutes ago. You're now facing a murder charge."

Fear, pure and unfiltered, pooled inside him and he saw his life flash before him. He'd spend the next twenty-five years in jail for defending his sister and putting some prick down for raping her. He began to breathe through his nose as the walls closed in on him and he tried not to puke.

"Breathe, Bram. Just breathe and listen to me. I can make all this go away."

That got Bram's attention from his predicament. "How and why?"

"I have the right contacts and can make sure this goes down as a random attack with an unknown assailant."

"There was a pub full of people who saw me drag him out."

"But only your friends saw you beat him, and they won't talk. You'll go into the army for a minimum of eight years and when you come out, you'll be given a choice to join my team or to go your own way."

"And what do you get out of this?"

"I get a highly trained elite soldier for my new team and someone who I know is willing to do what it takes to protect the innocent and isn't afraid to break a few rules to get it done."

"What makes you think I'd be any good at this? You don't even know me."

"I know you're top of your class and passed all your A-levels with Highers. I know you hate sushi but love smoked salmon. I know you eat with your knife and fork in the opposite hands to what is considered normal. I also know that you've been taking motorbike lessons behind your family's back and that you have a new tattoo of a birdcage on your left bicep. You also knew I was watching you and you've already clocked all the cameras in the room, including the one people aren't meant to know about."

Bram sat back, stunned into silence by the knowledge this man had and his observational skills.

"How did I do?"

"Who the fuck are you?"

"That doesn't matter. What I need to know is, are you in or out?"

Bram knew he had no choice but was intrigued to know why. "Why me?"

"You remind me of someone. I see good in you but also the potential to be the best."

"What about my sister?" Leaving Lana after everything she'd been through felt wrong.

"We'll see to it that she gets the best care and counselling to help her heal from her ordeal."

"I need to think about it."

"No, when I leave this room the offer leaves with me."

Bram had a chance to make his life right and to serve in the army, which had been a lifelong dream he'd thought would never be realised. His father was so set against it he'd stopped mentioning it and settled for his love of the outdoors as his passion; now his body was alight with the possibility of having a true purpose. Of making a difference to people's lives and futures. "I'm in."

The man nodded and stood, offering his hand to shake. "Welcome aboard. You can call me Jack."

With that, Jack led him out of the room and down the back corridor, passing three officers. As they reached the fire exit, the detective from earlier rounded the corner. Bram froze, thinking he was about to be hauled back into a cell, but the detective just nodded once and kept going. His life was about to change for the second time in less than twenty-four hours but this time he felt confident it was for the better.

CHAPTER 1

TEN YEARS LATER

BEIN HUNCHED LOWER INTO HIS LEATHER JACKET AS HE PULLED HIS COLLAR up to cover his neck. He'd thought, after being brought up in the Highlands, the cold wouldn't get to him, but the Black Mountains were cold as fuck on this October morning. Resetting the cameras that protected the place he called home should've been an easy task, but free climbing down an icy rock face was trickier than it looked. Good thing he was an adrenaline junkie and loved anything to do with climbing, bungee jumping, parachuting. If it was dangerous, Bein wanted to be involved.

Nestled on the Welsh border, the mountains made up part of the Brecon Beacons National Park. It reminded him of home, with the beautiful, almost wild landscape of the hills. Yet nobody knew that the Mountain Search and Rescue Centre that had set up on Black Hill just two miles north of the small village of Longtown was a front for what was the most secret black ops team in the world.

Bein stepped through the door to the centre and felt the warmth of the heating tickle his skin. He was used to the bite of the cold and knew it wouldn't be long before he was stripping his shirt off.

The woman behind the desk looked up and smiled at him.

"Hey, Snow." He ambled over and leaned on the counter that made up the main focus of the centre. In the back was everything they'd need for any kind of search and rescue mission and the front consisted of leaflets on local focal points and some safety guides. Snow was five foot nothing, petite with white-blonde hair and heather blue eyes. She'd been given the name because of her hair and how easily she could blend in with the snow and cold. A good thing for a former jewel thief.

"You drew the short straw today?" None of the team liked doing desk duty; public relations wasn't really in their wheelhouse.

"Fucking Bás has a bug up his ass about something and I made a comment about it, so I got desk duty."

Bein banged the desk with his hand and laughed. "You need to learn to keep your mouth shut."

"And you need to fuck off before I clock you one." Her French accent was always stronger when she was pissed, and she continued to mutter in French as he walked away chuckling. Snow was like an annoying younger sibling, full of energy and joy but boy did she have a temper on her when she was riled.

Moving past her, he went into the staff only quarters that accessed the true heart of the Shadow Elite operations and command centre. Using a retinal and palm scan, he stepped into the steel lift shaft that would take him hundreds of feet below the earth. It stopped with a smooth glide and he pressed his palm to the lift doors again to access the floor. It was an added safety measure in case someone ever tried to access the secure area.

He could hear voices as he walked into the well-lit corridor and headed in the direction of the offices. This facility also housed luxury living quarters kitted out for each member of the team as well as a war room where all the fun toys like grenade launchers and weapons were held, and a tech room, which was the domain of Watchdog, their resident technical genius and hacker. A large meeting room was next to the offices, and spare accommodation, including holding cells for any persons of interest they may need to detain.

He kept moving towards Bás' office, the leader of Shadow Elite and a complete badass enigma to them all. Which was saying a lot considering every member of the team had a history that had been wiped clean the second they signed on with Shadow.

He leaned his shoulder against the door frame of the open office door and Bás noticed him immediately.

"Get your ass in here."

Bein moved to sit next to Duchess. She was second in command at Shadow, and he knew she was ex-military but definitely not army because he'd never met her in his time. She was a good leader and more of a people person than Bás, which made them a good team. She was also stunningly beautiful, made all the more so by the array of tattoos on her body and neck. Anyone foolish enough to mistake her beauty and charm for weakness soon found out, the hard way, how wrong they were. She was deadly, silent, and better with a knife than anyone he'd ever met, except maybe Reaper.

Bás continued talking as if Bein had always been in on the conversation, leaving him to catch up. "Duchess, you continue working the Cavendish brothers, Jack wants that as a priority, and I agree. Carter Cavendish is getting out of hand with more bodies than ever turning up. I have a feeling if we keep pushing one of the brothers will turn."

"Agreed, Gideon is warier, but I think Damon is at the end of his rope. He wants to float the company and with the current stirrings it will affect the stock price."

"Good, work that angle but don't push too hard. We need him to trust you."

"Oh, he does, and he has a kink for my artwork. The more I say no, the more he wants me."

Bein shook his head, knowing Duchess loved the attention she got and the power it gave her over the men she worked.

Bás frowned and Bein knew he didn't like her getting so close to her target, but it was her call to make and her body.

"I want you to take Bishop and Reaper with you to London. They can work Carter and Gideon from the other angles."

"Sure."

Bein turned in his seat to see Lotus chewing her nail looking bored. He knew the nonchalance was fake though and she was taking in every word. Lotus had more history with Bás than anyone else on the team and she was a skilled killer and hunter, but not military. No, she had a much more interesting background. Beside her sat Titan, a giant of a black man who looked like he could and would kill you in a heartbeat and not break his stride, but he was probably the calmest of them all.

A former London gang leader, he'd been given a second chance and was making up for the wrongs he'd done by serving with Shadow. His path and outside influences had taken him places he regretted and turned him into someone he wasn't. Now he was almost zen in his search for redemption.

"Bein, I want you, Lotus, and Titan to keep searching for Joel Hansen. He's still in the wind and I don't fucking like it."

"I'll talk to some contacts and see if I can get a read on him." Lotus didn't look up from picking her nails and Bein knew it annoyed the shit out of Bás which was why she did it.

Some of the team hadn't only had their backgrounds wiped clean but their very existence. Titan and Lotus were both officially dead and so was Bás. The contacts they'd made had to be nowhere near their old stomping grounds in case they were recognised and their covers were blown.

Having a base under a mountain on the Welsh border certainly helped with that, and the locals all knew them as the mountain rescue people and called them by the names they'd chosen when their identities were wiped and new aliases had been put in place if someone went looking, like a nosey local copper.

He'd stuck with Bram, but his team all called him Bein, and he mostly used their code names too. They were tight, a team that had to rely on each other for their lives in deadly situations but also friendships. All of them lived in their quarters here and spent most evenings together or in their rooms if they wanted peace and quiet. It was like a dysfunctional fucking commune.

"I ken a clipe that might be able to help?"

"English, Bein, I don't speak fucking Jock."

Bein turned to Lotus who was glaring at him, and he smirked. "Haud yer wheesht, wench."

Telling her to shut up in any accent was a risky business but he knew she was looking for a fight and, as her friend, he was happy to give it to her. Plus, he fancied a sparring session to ease the tension and clear the cobwebs. It was coming up on the tenth anniversary of the night his sister was attacked, and it always made him antsy.

"You little dick."

Bein stood and winked. "Nothin' small about it, darlin'."

"Okay, enough. Get the fuck out of my office and get to work. I want a report on my desk by Friday morning."

Bein walked out with Duchess and a seething Lotus behind him with Titan.

"You really shouldn't wind her up you know."

"I know, but she needs a fight and I'm happy to give it to her."

Duchess nudged his shoulder with her own. "You're a good guy, Bein."

He wished that was true, but they all knew none of them were truly good. They'd seen and done too much for that to be true. "Lotus, I'll meet you in the ring in ten minutes."

"Bring it on, asshole."

Jogging back to his quarters, he let himself in using his seven-digit code. His rooms comprised of a living area, kitchen, bathroom, and bedroom. He'd decorated it how he wanted as it was likely to be the only home he'd ever have, or at least until he was no longer operational and then he'd see what happened and where his life led him.

He'd gone for blues and greens with a dark blue couch and tartan throw pillows because they reminded him of home. His kitchen was the same as the others, white and a high gloss with all the appliances he could possibly need. His bedroom had a king-size bed with a green quilt cover and fur throw.

It didn't happen often but if the generator went out and the backup generator came on, it could knock the heating out and then it was fucking freezing down there. He hated being over hot but being cold was just as bad.

Changing into gym shorts and a vest, he headed back to the gym area located next to the war room. Lotus was already in the ring, warming up. Titan was spotting the bench for Reaper and Hurricane, the last member of the team and one he knew from the military. Hurricane was ex-Air Force and had been one of the pilots to fly him and his team out of a high-risk zone after an IED attack had killed two of his teammates. Flying home via Germany with his friend's bodies, and knowing their families would never be the same again, had been the second hardest thing he'd ever done.

The first had been seeing his sister broken after her attack and knowing he was to blame. Bein shook the thought away. It did no good to drag up the past, just made him travel further down the dark path that led to his own personal hell. It was why he didn't forge relationships with people outside his team. He couldn't risk them getting hurt and tearing what was left of his heart apart.

Bein stopped a little ways away to watch Hurricane lift. He was benching a very impressive one hundred and seventy-five kilos currently and hardly sweating. Bein was strong, but not Hurricane strong. He was also six foot three of pure black muscle, as he liked to remind Bein. It was unusual for a pilot to be so big, but he loved his weights and it helped with his demons, whatever they were. Bein never asked and Hurricane never shared.

Climbing into the ring, he grinned at Lotus, who just glared and bounced around him before striking so fast he had no time to move. He landed on his back with a hard thud, blood trickling from his lip and grinned.

It was game on.

He never gave an inch as he and Lotus fought, each trying to gain the upper hand. With no rules, it was a dirty fight. Before this team, he'd never fought a woman and at first, it had been awkward as he hadn't wanted to hurt any of them and had been brought up to never lay a finger on a woman. After having his ass handed to him several times and realising these women were far from shrinking violets and could more than handle themselves, he'd got with the programme. He now treated them exactly like he would the men and learned a few techniques that he otherwise wouldn't have.

After an hour, he and Lotus were both sweating and bruised, but the tension in them both was gone. It wasn't as good as getting laid but that was strictly prohibited within the team, so that was a no go and he saw the women like sisters, not in any sexual way at all.

Bein grinned at his friend. "I'd say that's a draw, ya little bawbag."

"Will you stop with the romantic names. I told you I just don't see you that way."

Lotus was laughing as he slung his arm around her shoulder. He noogied her head with his knuckles, knowing full well that she knew bawbag wasn't romantic. "You're a pain in the arse."

"And you're a loser who owes me a drink."

"Fine."

He was unwrapping his knuckles as he approached the others. "Anyone want to go for a drink tonight?"

"Can't, man. I have to leave for London with the boss lady."

Reaper was ex-Australian special forces and looked like he'd just stepped off a surfboard with his blond hair and relaxed charm, but he didn't get the name Reaper by wearing a Halloween costume. He was deadly, and his kill ratio was high. There wasn't a target he couldn't hit. There was only one person better with a sniper rifle on the team and that was Bein.

Years hunting in the Scottish Highlands had made him skilled before he joined the military and they'd honed him into the best sniper the army had seen since Zack Cunningham had been up on the wall of fame. "We headed to The Crown?"

Titan rolled his eyes. "Is there anywhere else around here?"

He wasn't wrong. The Crown was the only pub in the town of Longtown that was close to them and owned by Bob Harris, a friend of Shadow who knew exactly who they were. Jack Granger had set the man up in business ten years ago when he'd been planning Shadow. Putting an ex-special forces guy in the local pub to help with their cover had been a good plan. If anyone came sniffing around, Bob was always the first to hear about it and gave them the heads up.

"Meet you in an hour up top. Make sure someone invites Snow. She looked a little fed up earlier."

"Ah, look at you being all caring and shit."

Bein gave Reaper the middle finger before he walked off to shower and change. Getting out tonight would be a good thing, because next week he had to deal with his family estate, and he wasn't looking forward to it.

CHAPTER 2

THE SOUND OF WOOD CRACKLING IN THE PUB'S LOG FIRE GREETED THEM AS Bein, Titan, and Lotus walked up to the bar. The pub was quintessentially British, from the brass taps to beer mats on the wall and it was a comfort on a cold night like this one. Bein nodded at Bob, who was talking to a local at the other end of the wooden bar and he waved back, acknowledging them. He was starving and one of Bob's steak and ale pies with creamy mash was just what he needed tonight. His head was buried in the menu deciding if he was going to have extra chips on the side when he heard a voice.

"What can I get you?"

He looked up and was met with the best pair of tits he'd seen in a long time, but that was nothing compared with the face that greeted him when he dragged his eyes upwards. He quickly averted his gaze from the plain purple tee, which shouldn't be sexy but, on this beauty, should be damn illegal.

Her eyebrows raised and he realised he'd been staring so long he'd forgotten the question. "Sorry, what?"

"What would you like to drink?"

"Oh, I'll have two pints of ale and a pint of Bulmer's Original, please."

He watched her begin pulling the pints with the ease of someone who'd been doing it for a long time. His eyes skimmed over tight fitted jeans that complimented her arse to perfection to her flat boots, which had seen better days but weren't cheap, which meant she must've had money at some point.

She had long dark hair that had red highlights through it when she moved her head and the firelight caught her just right, startling jade green eyes, pale skin, and if he wasn't very much mistaken, an Irish accent that she was trying very hard to hide.

Closing the menu, he concentrated on the woman who was moving around the bar with ease, but he noticed she never once turned her back on him or anyone else in the room. Fascinated, Bein took in her frame, which was thin despite the all-natural curves that weren't from some weird injections or filler.

Her eyes wouldn't meet his as she placed his drinks on the bar mat in front of him. She seemed shy, hesitant, hyper-aware of her surroundings. "That'll be ten pounds, fifty-seven pence, please."

Bein handed over a twenty and she quickly turned to the cash register to get his change, again keeping the door and the patrons in sight. Someone in the pub dropped a glass and as it smashed, she jumped, her whole body tensing, her terrified eyes moving to the door looking for an escape before she realised what it was and visibly relaxed her shoulders.

She moved to hand him his change and he held his hand up. "Keep it, darlin'."

"Are you sure? That's a lot."

"Yeah, you have a drink yourself."

"Thank you, that's very kind." Still, she didn't meet his eyes.

He watched her put the change in the tip jar, which he knew would be shared out among the other members of staff at the end of the week. "You're not from around here, are ya?"

She gave him a deer in the headlights look before dropping her eyes in a way that made his dick sit up and take notice. His thoughts immediately went to her on her knees looking up at him through those long sexy lashes in a submissive position. God, he needed to get laid, and soon, if he was fantasising about terrified barmaids.

"No. How do you know that?"

"Relax, darlin', I work at the search and rescue centre so know most people around these parts, plus this is my local and I certainly would've remembered a beauty like you."

Usually, he didn't have to work to get a woman interested but this one fell flat, and she just shook her head. "I need to get on."

She walked away to refill the crisps and he was left with so many questions about this woman. Only one person could answer them, and he was still busy yammering. That was the thing with Bob, he loved to gossip so much he was like an old woman.

Walking towards his friends, he set the three pints down, handing Titan his cider and Lotus her ale.

He sat, took a long pull on the pint, and wiped the foam from his upper lip. He saw his friends smirking and frowned. "What?"

Titan shrugged. "Nothing, just never seen you strike out before. It's refreshing."

"Fuck off. I didn't even flirt with her."

"Oh, you definitely flirted with her, and she shut your ass down." Lotus was trying not to laugh louder.

"I wasn't giving her my A-game and anyway, she seems too shy for me. Plus, she's hiding something, and I don't need that kind of drama."

Titan held up his pint in salute. "Yep, totally get it, man."

Lotus was playing with a spare beer mat, twirling it between her fingers as if it was a throwing star. "So, what are your thoughts on Hansen?"

"Honestly, I think this guy has gone to ground, and until he pokes his head above the parapet, we're on a hiding to nothing."

"I agree, but we have to try. This is personal for Jack and Eidolon after what he did to Astrid and Adeline. This dick deserves to die for what he's done. Plus, I owe Jack more than I can ever repay."

Bein didn't know the full story, just that Lotus had been involved with the wrong people and Jack had given her a second chance.

Titan sat back in his chair, folding his hands over his chest. "Jack gave me back my self-worth, and for that, he'll always have my loyalty."

"I think we can all agree that Jack is the reason we're here and not washed-up, dead, or in jail, but this is going to be a long game of cat and mouse with Hansen. We need to play smart, not fast. See through the chaos instead of allowing this prick to play us."

A movement to his right had him turning to see the new barmaid laughing with old man Johnson. He had to be as old as these fucking mountains and yet he was still out on the hills day and night, checking his sheep that roamed free. Her laugh was deep and husky. Real, not fake and tinkly like some women who did it for attention.

It made him wonder what he'd said to get that reaction. She must have felt him looking because she glanced up and the spark between them arced across the room, leaving him aching to talk to her, to kiss her and feel her skin before she broke the connection and looked swiftly away. It was a strange reaction to someone he hardly knew and not one he'd had before. Chemistry was a strange thing and they clearly had it in spades.

"Did you order the food? I'm starving?" Lotus complained.

"Ah, shit. I totally forgot." Bein jumped up and went to the bar, where Bob had finished gassing finally.

"Hey, lad. What can I get ya?"

"Can I get a steak and ale pie with mash and extra gravy, a chicken curry with rice, chips, and extra poppadums, and fish and chips with mushy peas, please?"

"That everything?"

"Yeah, thanks, Bob."

Bein handed over the cash and waited for his change, using the opportunity to watch the new girl. Bob handed him his change. "Thanks. So, tell me about the new girl?"

Bob glanced across at her, as did he, as she began restocking the soft drinks. She knew they were talking about her; he saw her back stiffen ever so slightly, her awareness heightened as she angled her head as if trying to listen. She'd never hear over the noise of the patrons in the pub, but the fact she was so scared affected him in a way that made him uneasy. She was slim, probably too slim, and always moving as if she couldn't keep still.

"She came in a few weeks ago looking for some cash-in-hand work. I wouldn't normally do it, but you know sometimes you get a vibe that someone is in trouble and needs help, and that's her."

"You think she's in some kind of trouble?"

Bob looked at him through narrowed eyes, slowly nodding. "I think she's running or hiding. Probably both and whatever it is she's running from has her jumping at shadows and I don't like that. She's a good girl, works hard, is polite and friendly, the customers like her, and you know this lot don't normally warm to strangers easily."

Bein did know that. It had taken them almost a year to accept him. He didn't like the idea of this woman being afraid, it didn't sit right with him at all. "She got a name?"

"She told me it's Debbie, but when I say her name, she doesn't answer to it very quick. I think that's a lie too, but she has her reasons and as long as she does the work and plays by the rules then I've no problem with her keeping her business to herself."

"Want me to get Watchdog to run her?"

"Nah, let her be."

"Okay." Bein didn't exactly agree with that decision, but it was Bob's to make.

He headed back to the table, grabbing knives and forks and condiments as he went. This wasn't the kind of establishment that did table service.

Titan lifted a curved eyebrow. "Well?"

Bein dumped the stuff in the middle of the table for them to help themselves. "Well, what?"

"What did Bob have to say about the new girl?" He held a hand up to stop Bein. "And please don't embarrass yourself by denying it."

"Why are you always busting my ass, guys?"

"Because it's fun," Lotus replied.

"You're all assholes but fine, yes I asked. Her name is Debbie, and he thinks she's running from something or someone."

"Yeah, and if her name is Debbie, mine's the Virgin Mary."

Lotus' real name was actually Nazareli Holt but only a select few ever called her Naz.

"Exactly, he said the same. I asked if he wanted us to look into it, but he didn't so..." Bein shrugged one shoulder.

"Probably a dickhead ex-boyfriend."

"Or girlfriend. Not only men can be psychos, you know." Titan defended his sex.

"Fine, whatever. Either way, it isn't our problem unless lover boy gets involved."

"I'm not getting involved. I just think she's fit, and I wouldn't mind fucking her, that's all."

A throat cleared and he glanced behind him to see Debbie with their food balanced on her arms. He didn't want to think of her by Debbie because he knew it was a lie—he'd much prefer to think of her as Irish so that was what he'd do. Her face was bright red, and he knew she'd heard him. He glared at Lotus knowing she'd done it on purpose.

Irish laid the plates on the table and linked her fingers behind her back, rocking back on her heels. "Can I get you guys anything else?"

"Can I get some ketchup, please?" Lotus asked.

Irish looked at him and then Titan, her eyes flitting away quickly. "What about you guys?"

"Nah, I'm good."

Bein nodded his agreement and watched her head back to get the ketchup.

"Not cool, Lotus."

"But fun."

"Don't play with her. She isn't your toy." His words were harsher than he intended but he didn't regret that. Lotus was lovely but she could be hard and a little abrasive until a person got to know her, and sometimes forgot people didn't always get her humour.

She stopped with a chip halfway to her mouth in surprise at his outburst. "You're right, I'm sorry."

Bein nodded. "It's cool."

That was the thing with Lotus, she could be a bit of hard work, but she was always quick to say if she was wrong.

When Irish set the ketchup down and smiled as she went to walk away, Lotus stopped her.

"Hey, I'm sorry about embarrassing you back there. It wasn't cool, and I shouldn't have done it."

Irish rubbed her hands together in a nervous gesture, but her shoulders were back in a confident manner, and he was intrigued by the fact she was a bunch of contradictions.

"No, it wasn't cool but we all have off days. So, apology accept-ed." Irish smiled wide and walked away head high even though he could see her glancing around as she did.

"I think I like her."

Lotus grinned and he knew standing up to Lotus was a good thing and would make her respect her more. Not that he cared. He couldn't get involved with her, he had too many plates to juggle already, even if she was fucking beautiful.

CHAPTER 3

Bob shooed her out of the bar as she wiped down the last of the tables. "Get yourself home, lassie. I can close up from here."

It had been a busy night for midweek, especially for a bar in a small village but like most small pubs it had its regulars, and she was slowly getting to know them. "Thanks, Bob."

Aoife gathered her bag and the jacket she needed to upgrade to a winter one very shortly and headed into the darkness. She could feel a migraine coming on from the familiar tightness around her eyes and the stabbing pain in her head and knew she needed to get home before it completely took her out.

The night and darkness had never bothered her. It had been the days when her life had been a nightmare. Now, though, as she walked along the narrow lanes from the pub to the small flat she'd rented from Mrs Jones above the bakery, the pitch-black was unnerving. Every shadow held the possibility of her being snatched back into the life she'd almost died to get away from.

Nausea rolled in her belly and her vision became spotty as the pain began to pulse harder and harder. Her steps became more uncoordinated as her body started to shut down in a way to protect her from the pain. She needed her pills and her bed, fast, or she'd be out for days, and she couldn't afford that. Aoife needed to save every penny she could so she had money to run and start again at the drop of a hat.

Thankful that the night held no bright lights, she quickened her step. In the city, there was always light from a house or streetlights but out here in the countryside, it was only the moon and the stars to guide her. Thank God for her torch which she used to navigate her way, even if the light from it was making her feel sicker.

The sounds of owls calling and hooting, foxes shouting, which sounded like women screaming and made chills run up her spine, sounded louder to her pain-filled brain. Yet, she could still admire the beauty of this place against the backdrop of the beautiful hills where sheep roamed free, and nature was allowed to flourish. Exhaustion was making her emotional, fear and the pounding in her head making her extra jumpy.

The three strangers from the bar had set off every radar she had, her brain screaming danger, the fight or flight response so strong it took everything she had not to run out of the bar.

Only seeing Bob talking to them with so much friendly familiarity had eased her worry and allowed her to continue her shift. As the night wore on, she'd felt his eyes on her, the man with the scar on his eyebrow and the tattoos covering his hands and neck, but his blue eyes didn't hold the dead evil she'd come to recognise. She had no doubt in her mind that those three were more than they seemed, maybe even killers but they weren't a threat to her. At least she hoped not, or she was already dead.

Rounding the last bend, she heard a branch snap behind her and stilled, her whole body freezing as she looked back. Seeing nothing but the still night she began to jog, as much as her body would allow, wanting to get into the semi-safe confines of her tiny flat. Knowing she would never be safe again was a weight that grew heavier with each day that passed, yet she wouldn't give it up and go back to the prison she'd been in before.

When the key slid into the lock and she was safely inside, she leaned against the door and took a deep breath. Leaving the lights off, she stumbled into her small bedroom and sank onto the bed. Grabbing the pain killers from the bedside drawer she swallowed them back dry and hoped she'd taken them quickly enough.

Her belly rumbled but she knew food was the last thing she needed, even though she hadn't eaten since breakfast. Shrugging off her coat Aoife lay back on her bed and closed her eyes for just a second. She knew it was time to check her messages, the time and date were always the same so Peyton, her only friend in the world who knew where she was, could get information to her.

Thinking of her friend, who was a PTSD therapist who specialised in military personnel, always made her smile. They'd gone to a Catholic boarding school together and stayed friends after-wards, and it was the only true friendship she had. She was the only person on the planet Aoife trusted. Peyton was the opposite of her in looks, she was blonde with a sexy girl next door vibe, a body to die for, pale blue almost grey eyes, and a nature that drew people to her. She had been the one who'd helped Aoife escape the hell she'd been living through.

Sitting up slowly, she swung her legs off the bed and took out her phone from under her mattress. Sliding in the battery and sim card, she gave it a second to power on and saw two messages from her friend.

Her gut dropped as it was unusual for her and she braced herself to read them. It had only been six months of running and she was already exhausted from it. At twenty-five, she felt like she was a hundred years old. The physical injuries she carried from her father, including the migraines that plagued her, the result of a head injury when she was fifteen, were nothing compared to the emotional and psychological scars.

Peyton had tried for years to counsel her through making a choice to leave her home, but she'd stayed for her mother, not wanting her to shoulder the burden alone. When she'd died five years ago, Aoife had wanted desperately to leave but her father wasn't an idiot and had tightened her security so that she was never alone, a guard with her at all times.

Knowing she couldn't avoid the messages all night, she clicked the first.

P: I HAD A VISIT FROM YOUR FATHER TODAY. HE WAS ASKING IF I'D SEEN YOU OR HEARD FROM YOU. I TOLD HIM I HADN'T BUT I'M NOT SURE HE BELIEVED ME. STAY WHERE YOU ARE, HE DOESN'T KNOW YOU'RE CLOSE.

Aiofe gasped, a sob trying to break free, as cold and pure fear knotted hard in her belly. If her father was in Hereford that meant he'd tracked her somehow. Tears stung her eyes as she tried to hold herself together. Breaking down would get her nowhere, no matter how much she wanted to. She looked at the next message that had come in twenty minutes later.

P: I HAD A FRIEND TRACK YOUR FATHER AND HE'S HEADED TOWARDS BRISTOL, SO I HAD THEM LEAVE A TRAIL FOR HIM. DON'T WORRY, I DIDN'T TELL HIM WHO IT WAS FOR, BUT YOU CAN TRUST HIM. CALL ME WHEN YOU CAN. I MISS YOU.

Aiofe blinked back more tears, knowing her friend was trying to help, but in doing so she was taking such a risk. If her father ever found out, he wouldn't think twice about killing Peyton, and none of her friends who she thought could protect her would be able to, not from Jimmy Doyle, her father and leader of the Irish Mafia.

The thought of her dad hurting Peyton made her sick, but she didn't know where to turn or who to trust. The long fingers of the Irish mafia had seeped through into organisations here. She could go to the Italians or the Russians and ask them for help. It would be a coup to have the only daughter of Jimmy Doyle on their side, but it could just as easily go the other way and she could find herself out of the frying pan into the fire.

Taking out the sim and battery, she stowed her phone away and lay back down on her bed. She should get undressed, but her energy was flagging, and the pain relief had only taken the edge off, so she still felt wretched.

Dragging her ass to the bathroom, she stripped her clothes and folded them into a bag so she could wash them the next day. Pulling on her pink penguin pyjamas, she looked in the mirror and wondered where the girl who was never seen without make-up and a full set of nail extensions had gone. Seeing the pale skin and dark shadows under her eyes, she barely recognised herself. Even the jade of her eyes, her best feature, seemed dull. She was tired, and it wasn't the kind of tiredness that could be fixed with a good night's sleep, although that would be heaven. No, this was an exhaustion that was bone-deep and she knew depression was creeping in and would take her down and, with it, her ability to run. She needed a proper plan to fix this or she was as good as dead.

Plodding back to bed, she knew the thing she needed most right now was sleep and to get rid of her migraine. Snuggling under the quilt, she listened to the sounds of the countryside as she closed her eyes. In here, the animal sounds seemed less scary; this had become her sanctuary over the last few weeks.

Something about this village and these people made her feel safe, and the fact they spotted a stranger so quickly meant her father's men couldn't go around hunting for her unspotted without rattling the locals. Bob hadn't questioned her name or story, but she knew he saw through it and had helped her anyway. He was a good guy, and she got a nice vibe off him. He was like the father she wished she'd had.

As her mind cycled through the evening, her way of winding down enough to sleep, she stalled on the sexy hunk with tattoos and a leather jacket. He'd come in with a big, muscular black man and a smaller woman with dark hair. All three gave off a dangerous vibe as if it emanated from their very pores like electricity. Yet, she hadn't been afraid, not like she was around her father's men.

Far from fear, the sex god at the bar who'd been flirting with her had made her remember how long it had been since she'd had sex, along with a desire she'd never thought she'd feel again after every-thing she'd been through. The last had been a guy from the village where her grandmother lived and they'd been visiting. He'd died three days later in a car accident, which she knew very well was her father's doing. She'd thought the horror that followed had killed that part of her and it was a relief and shock to feel anything for a man.

Tattoos weren't normally her thing, and the guy from the bar tonight had been covered in them, even his neck and hands were inked. But he had kind eyes, which twinkled, and a strong Scottish accent which she found as sexy as sin. Dark blond, hair which had firelight reds in it was longer on top and short at the sides. It looked soft and she'd wanted to run her fingers through it.

It had been a long time since she'd wanted anyone and the chemistry between them was immediate and intense, but she tamped it down, knowing no good could come from it. Even if she tried, she'd probably choke with fear and humiliate herself. Even if a short fling might be a good distraction from the misery of her life, it was a bad idea.

His friends had been colourful, the woman having a caustic streak which Aoife could appreciate for what it was; a way to put up barriers. Her apology had been genuine though, and Aoife thought perhaps had been instigated by the guy who she couldn't stop thinking about now.

Sleep that night was fitful but when she did sleep sexy blue eyes filled her dreams instead of the usual one where she was running through mud and couldn't move.

CHAPTER 4

Bás looked up from the report Bein placed on his desk and raised his eyebrow, clearly unimpressed with what he was reading. "Nothing! That tells me exactly nothing."

Bein sank down into the chair opposite his boss and leaned back. He'd known Bás wouldn't like this, but the truth was Hansen was a master at disappearing and was a slippery little bastard to boot. "You know damn well that he has the vast resources of the Agency at his disposal and unless he raises his head again, we're not helping anyone wasting our time searching for him. As I said in my report," Bein nodded at the three-page report he'd written this morning, "the best option is to have fail-safes in place so that if he pokes his head out, we can take him out."

Bás looked back at the report, and he knew his boss would see the sense in what he was saying—he just didn't like it. Which was unusual for him. He was normally the long-game player and patient as fuck but with this case, he obviously wanted Hansen more than he'd originally let on.

"What's this about, Bás?"

The hierarchy in Shadow Elite was more relaxed than the army.

They were a tight unit and when it was time for a mission, leadership was followed without question in the field. Here in this room, he could question Bás with no repercussions but ultimately the final word was with Bás.

"He has information I need for a personal matter."

Bein sat forward. "Anything I can help with?"

"No."

"Well, I'm here if you need anything."

"Appreciate it. Now set those protocols up so we don't miss this bastard. He's not to slip through the net again."

"Sure, thing. I'll talk to Watchdog and have him set them up today."

He went to walk away but Bás stopped him. "Bein?"

"Yeah?"

"You going to sort your parents' estate next week?"

"Yeah. Should take about a week or so. Lana has done a lot of it but it's not fair to make her do it all. She's six months pregnant with her fifth child."

"Wow, I know you live in the asshole of nowhere but is there no TV in the Highlands?"

Bein blanched, his face clearly showing his distaste. "Dude, that's my sister."

Bás laughed and stood to follow him out, clapping him on the shoulder as he did. "You need any help, you shout, okay? I know it was tough between you and your dad for a long time."

"It was but he was still my dad, and although I hated some of his choices, I loved him. Not sure I'd be who I am today without him. Not that he ever knew it."

"Family is the single hardest relationship of your life."

"I thought that was marriage."

"No clue about that, but, if you get a bad wife, you can always divorce her. If you get shitty family, you're kinda stuck with them."

"Pretty sure you're not meant to go into marriage thinking about divorce."

"Good job I ain't getting hitched then."

"True."

"You gonna take over your dad's title now?"

Bein shook his head, "No, Shadow is my life. Lana runs the estate with her husband perfectly well without me."

"You know Jack would give you your life back if you wanted it, don't you?"

"Yeah, I know that, but I'm not that person anymore. Lana loves the life and the estate and so do her kids. I'm happy to keep the title and if my sons ever want it, they can have it or not, but it's hers to run and live in for her lifetime."

It's the least I can do for her after the way I failed her.

"Kids? Fuck, you knocked someone up?"

"God no. But maybe one day, never say never." He glanced at Bás. "You want kids and a family?"

Bás shook his head. "Nah, not for me. I'd be a shit father. I'm too selfish."

Bein lifted his chin in response because he didn't necessarily agree but who was he to tell him that. He couldn't even manage his own love life let alone have an opinion on someone else's life. If he was honest, he wasn't sure kids were in his future either. He never wanted to feel the kind of grief losing his friends had evoked in him again, and the thought of a daughter of his going through what Lana had made him want to kill, to drag Ray Walsh from the grave so he could kill the fucker all over again. Perhaps he'd leave kids and family to his sister. She was more than filling the family quota for offspring.

They walked toward the living quarters, which was quiet at this time of day, the team either out on a mission or beginning to chill for the evening. They kept odd hours. It definitely wasn't a nine to five job, and he knew they'd all go stir crazy in an environment like that.

"I'm gonna catch up on Walking Dead and drown myself in expensive whisky and frozen pizza."

"Sounds like a winning combination."

He kept walking when Bás stepped into his room which was opposite his own quarters. The living part of the compound was set out in a U shape, with a common room at the end where they could hang out together if they wanted. No expense or thought had been spared on this place. Jack had wanted the team who lived and worked here to be comfortable and happy and live as normal a life as he could make happen.

He loved it for the most part, but tonight he was twitchy and couldn't settle, and he knew the exact reason why. She was petite and sexy with a fake name and lyrical seductive laugh. Despite his pep talk with himself last night about not needing the hassle, he couldn't stop himself from throwing his jacket back on and heading to the pub.

He was acting totally out of character, he didn't fawn over women, he never had. Bein had always been easy come, easy go, no feelings or emotions, just some hot sex and then he kissed them as he walked out the door. Relationships led to commitment, and he couldn't give anyone that, not with his job and more importantly he didn't want to, either. Yet the second he'd laid eyes on Irish, something had happened, a spark, a feeling of knowing she would change everything, that she needed him.

He shook his head at the rambling thoughts that were so unlike him. He was happy to play the joker and was loyal to his friends, but he didn't need anyone else in his life to make him vulnerable. He had enough with his sister breeding over and over and making such adorable kids he couldn't help but love. The last thing he needed was a damsel in distress to save. Yet, something told him deep down the motion was already in play and he was a bystander with no control and that was unacceptable.

Scanning the lane as he walked from the rescue centre to the pub, he spied the house that Shadow used as a cover. Once a week, one or two of them would stay there to make it look like they either lived there in a shared house or stayed above the centre. It would be too suspicious for none of them to live around the area, plus it was good for them to have somewhere they could take someone if they hooked up.

Stepping into the warm atmosphere, he took in the room until his gaze landed on the woman who'd been on his mind all day. Her eyes met his across the bar and a small tentative smile creased her features, making him feel warm all over, his body tingling with something he couldn't put his finger on. It was like desire, but more as if he felt it in his chest as well as his dick.

He took a seat at the bar and waited for her to finish serving Bill Nevins who owned the sheep farm next to old man Johnson. The two bickered like a pair of fish wives but if one was in need the other would always help out. That was the way this community worked, and Irish seemed to be fitting in just perfectly with them.

He saw her walk towards him, her hips swaying in a way that was totally natural, none of it for show, just the gentle, sexy movement that had his mind going places it shouldn't in a room full of people mostly over sixty.

"What can I get ya?"

"I'll have a pint of Stowford's please."

Irish moved, smoothly pulling the pint, and placing it on the mat in front of him. Bein handed her the cash and she put it in the register. He watched her as he slowly sipped his cider. She seemed less jumpy, her movements less jerky, and she was smiling at Nevins and Johnson as they argued over some new legislation on sheep farming. Which was hilarious because he knew they agreed, they just liked to fight. She still watched the room though, as if she was waiting for someone to walk in and hoping they wouldn't.

With half an ear he listened to the two men bicker, his eyes on the beauty who moved with such grace. In this part of the country, and the deeper you went into Wales, sheep farms were everywhere. It wasn't unusual for drivers to have to stop their car and wait for a flock of sheep to move out of the way or see them grazing on the side of the mountain roads.

She moved closer to him as she polished a glass.

"These two are like an old married couple," he said getting Irish's attention.

She wore her hair down tonight and he loved how he caught the scent of her shampoo when she moved. He wondered how it would feel brushing against his chest as she rose over him, sinking down onto his length. Jesus, he was acting like a lovesick schoolboy, and he couldn't even remember being this wet when he was a boy with hormones raging through him so bad he'd had repetitive stress in his wrist from jerking off. He needed to dial it back, get to know her and find out if she was worth the effort. His dick had already made his vote clear, but he was in charge here.

"They're hilarious. Better than any comedy club. I get to watch them for free and get paid."

Bein sipped his pint. "You been to many comedy clubs?"

She tensed fractionally before he saw her relax. "A few."

Interesting. She was being vague, and nondescript and he agreed with Bob's assessment wholeheartedly. This woman was scared and running, which meant he should stay far away, get up from his seat and walk away. He did none of those things.

"Name's Bram but most people call me Bein, nice to meet you...?"

He held out his hand and waited a beat for her to take it. When she did, sparks shot from their joined palms up his arm and straight to his cock. Awareness shot between them, and her eyes went from jade green to emerald. She was fucking stunning, and he wanted her more than his next breath. Irish pulled her hand away and wiped it against her jeans as if trying to erase the sensation he knew she'd felt.

"Bein. That's an interesting name, but I prefer Bram and it's nice to meet you, too."

"Bein means mountain in Gaelic. I love the mountains and spend a lot of time there, so that was how I got the name Bein."

He waited for her to respond with her own name but she didn't, so he prompted her.

"You got a name or am I gonna call you Irish, princess?"

Her back snapped straight and he saw her pale before his eyes at his words. Her hand shook as she placed the glass on the rack, her eyes not meeting his and he saw true terror in her body language. It took everything in him not to drag her across the bar and hold her in his arms and tell her she was safe, but he didn't. She was nothing to him and Shadow couldn't afford for him to go around playing hero to random women, no matter how much he wanted to.

"W...why would you call me that?"

"Because you have an Irish accent?" He shrugged, trying to appear nonchalant when he felt anything but and took a sip of his drink as if he hadn't just seen her react the way he had. She needed to think she was getting things past him or she'd bolt, he could sense it.

"Oh, okay that makes sense and yeah call me Irish."

"So, Irish, important question, and this is very serious." He saw her take a small step back as he leaned forward, her trust in him as thin as rice paper.

"Okay," she responded slowly, drawing the word out.

"Ketchup or brown sauce on a bacon roll?"

Her smile lit up the room and Bein felt her relax as she leaned in closer again, the perceived threat she'd seen in him was suddenly gone now he was asking random questions.

"Brown sauce."

Bein gave her a grin and a wink and saw her flourish under his friendly banter. Maybe friends was what she needed more than a quick fuck, and he found himself wanting to get to know her better. "Good answer. Okay, next one. Apple pie or apple crumble?"

"Crumble, always crumble."

"Wow, you're smashing this."

"My turn."

He nodded, loving how she was opening up to him, even if she didn't realise it. As the night wore on, and in between serving punters, she stayed at the bar near him, and they continued to chat about mundane things. Movies, music, she was into Marvel movies, which he also loved, but hated horrors, which he didn't mind. She loved sushi, which he thought of as the devil's food, but they both loved sweet and salty popcorn rather than the toffee kind.

He found out she was well educated with a love of history and languages. That she loved Taylor Swift and hated Rap music. He told her he was ex-army, which was what he told everyone, sticking as close to the truth as he could about what he did in the past was always best. Most lies were based in truth, it was more authentic and made it easier to keep up the façade.

He glanced down at her ring finger and saw no marks but asked anyway. "You married, Irish?"

As soon as he said the words, the tension was back, the personal questions were where the danger lay for her, and it made him want to know more.

"No, not married. You?"

"No, I was married to the army and now my job here."

"So, what do you do exactly?"

Irish tucked a lock of hair behind her ear as she leaned in closer, her breasts pushing up and giving him a glimpse of the sexy curves under her conservative blue shirt. What made her more alluring was the fact she wasn't trying to be. Her only make-up was mascara and lip gloss, her clothes were conservative by most people's standards and hers was natural as far as he could tell. No cans of product holding every tendril in place. She was just herself and he wanted her badly.

She fancied him too, he could tell by the way her eyes moved over him and the pulse in her neck throbbed when he brushed his fingers over hers when she handed him a drink. Her guard was slowly coming down, but he knew he couldn't rush it.

"Well, we rescue people who get into trouble on the mountain, mainly walkers and hikers."

"What about the rest of the time?" She angled her head in a flirty manner, her focus on him instead of the people around her for the first time all night. She was relaxing and it was a beautiful thing to see.

"We train hard to stay fit and up to date with the latest news, and we sometimes go abroad when we're needed. We run training courses for other groups and teach safe wilderness techniques for staying alive if you get into trouble."

"What about you? You always want to be a barmaid?" Bein knew he needed to push her just a little and see if she opened up or shut down.

"Honestly?"

Bein chuckled. "No, lie to me. Of course honestly."

"Hey, don't be cheeky." Her smile faded. "Don't laugh, okay?"

Bein placed his hand over his heart. "Scout's honour."

Irish arched her brow and crossed her arms over her ample breasts, making his eyes drop as a groan escaped him making her blush and drop her arms.

"Come on, tell me before I do something stupid like jump over that bar and kiss you."

He saw interest light her eyes as her cheeks pinked up on her porcelain skin. "I wanted to be a nurse."

"Why is that funny?" He couldn't understand but knew it was something to do with why she was running.

She gave an awkward shrug. "It's not, I guess. It was just never something my family encouraged or would've allowed."

"Well, families are tricky, and we don't get to choose. My father nearly went doolally when I joined the army."

A defeated tone entered her voice as she spoke. "You're braver than me."

"Nah, ye just need to believe in yourself, darlin'." He could see his words hit the mark, but whoever had done such damage to her self-confidence had won this round. She wanted to believe what he said was true, but the fact was she didn't. But she would. If he had any say in it, she'd reach for the stars and touch them.

He could see her watching his lips as he spoke. "Your accent is hot."

Bein laughed at the compliment and smiled at her, letting her change the subject. He liked this girl. "Aye, so's yours."

Looking around, he realised the pub was empty and Bob was cleaning away some of the tables.

"I need to help Bob."

"Sure. Can I walk you home?"

"It's only down the road."

"Still, can I or not? The thought of you alone in the dark don't sit right with me."

"And what do you think happens when you aren't around?"

Bein didn't want to think about that, because her being alone and vulnerable didn't sit well with him at all. "I'm here now."

"Fine."

He helped Bob and Irish clean up, chatting with Bob about everyday happenings, but he could see the warning look the older man was giving him and understood exactly what it was. A warning to treat Irish with respect and he had no intention of doing anything else.

CHAPTER 5

Stepping out into the cool night felt completely different from twenty-four hours ago when she'd felt like the world was against her. The sexy man leaning on the low wall of the pub carpark was watching her with hunger in his eyes and there was nothing she wanted more than to be devoured by him, but that wasn't her life now or then, and never would be.

Waking this morning she'd felt so alone, despite the kindness of people around her and Peyton, who was going above and beyond to keep her safe. Still, lingering loneliness weighed her down. The simple act of hugging another person or talking and being part of something was what she missed the most.

"Which way?"

"The flat above the bakery."

"Lucky you. Those little petite fours Mrs Jones makes are heavenly." Bram kissed his fingers with a dramatic flair making her laugh.

Her eyes moved over him as they walked. He'd grabbed her hand and tingles drifted up her arm at the contact and it felt good. His touch felt right, natural. She noticed he was a pretty tactile guy, and she wasn't used to physical affection from a man that didn't lead to sex or violence, but she found his holding her hand both sweet and sexy. They walked in silence, the sexual tension beginning to fizzle between them the closer they got to her home.

"What part of Ireland are you from, Irish?"

Her body tensed. Any talk of home or hint at her past could lead to her father finding her and she just couldn't risk it. But how did she tell this normal, sexy guy, who she found attractive, that she was on the run from the most feared and dangerous man in Ireland?

Sensing her unease, he squeezed her hand. "You don't have to tell me, Irish, but just know you can trust me."

"It's not that, I just... I can't okay. Trust is a luxury few people have and I'm not one of them."

"Okay new question. Black liquorice. Yay or nay?"

Aoife smiled, how she wished things were different—that she could fall for a man like Bram and live happily ever after. Perhaps she could be selfish and take tonight. "A definite nay for me."

"Me too. I like the red kind though."

"Yeah, me too."

When she'd woken up that morning, Aoife had no intention of following through on her attraction to this man but now all she could think about were his lips on hers. How his body would feel under her hands, how he'd feel sliding into her body.

She stopped at the door to her flat and looked at him. Neither spoke for a moment as they looked at each other and then he was kissing her, pushing her against the door with power and strength. His heated lips exploring as her hands glided over the hard muscle of his chest, taking in the ridges and dips under her fingers. There was no fear, no danger or worry, only sensation and need.

Bram hummed in what she hoped was pleasure, his body tightening under her touch as Aoife's hands moved over his arms and down his back. He pulled his mouth away with a groan, before leaning down, finding the sweet pulse in her neck that made her shiver with need. This was reckless and stupid and in that moment she didn't care. She was sick of running scared, of avoiding life for fear of the consequences. Tonight, she wanted to take.

Bram's tattoos were barely visible in the darkness, but she could see the shadows and the images in her mind, the vision and feel of him making her ache to feel him inside her.

"Tell me to stop, Irish, or let me the fuck inside you."

His aggressive tone and the desperate way he wanted her made her feel powerful and desirable for the first time in her life and it was a heady feeling, to know she'd made a man like him, with so much control, snap. "Yes, I want you."

Aoife spun towards the front door. Feeling Bram pressed against her back, his hard cock rocking against the curve of her ass as his lips continued the assault on her neck, making it tricky to get the key in the lock.

"Fuck, you make me crazy." His voice was deep, raspy with desire, and made Aoife hungry for him.

As she got the door open, they fell inside, the door slamming with a kick of Bram's foot. Grabbing her he lifted, squeezing her ass with his huge hands as she wrapped her legs around his waist before he carried her up the stairs. Her lips found his and she could almost taste the lust on his tongue as it caressed hers in an intimate move that imitated what she wanted him to do to her body.

"Where?"

"Bedroom."

Aoife pointed to the closed door, and he headed that direction, his steps sure and confident, with her wrapped around him like a second skin. Bram sat on the edge of the bed and she stayed straddling him, her pussy rubbing against his hard dick, the seam of her jeans teasing them both as they continued to kiss. He pulled his head away and looked at her like she was the only woman on the planet and her nipples peaked with the intensity of the lust in his ice-blue eyes.

"You're fucking beautiful."

Aoife had nothing to say to that, so she kissed him, sucking his tongue, nipping his lip, her hands moving to his fly and releasing his hard cock from the confines of his jeans and boxers. Aoife gripped him, stroking the silky skin, her fingers hardly able to close around his thick length, rubbing her thumb over the precum on the crown causing Bram to throw his head back on a hiss.

"Fuck me."

Aoife chuckled. "That's the plan."

Bram let her be in charge for a minute, but she knew he was dying to take over. She could tell he loved control. She didn't know how she knew that, but she did.

As she ground against him, seeking that pleasure she'd only ever found on her own, her hand continued stroking his cock. Bram pulled her shirt open, the buttons popping and landing everywhere in the silence of the room, filled only with the sounds of moaning and whimpers. She'd be hunting for those later but right now she didn't care. All she wanted were his hands on her fevered skin, easing the ache that was blistering in its intensity.

Bram's eyes landed on her tits, and he rubbed a calloused thumb over each pebbled nipple, making her arch into him, a moan in her throat. Pulling down the cups on her bra, he let her breasts sit high, like a prize waiting to be claimed and he wasted no time doing it. His mouth sucked her nipple hard, his teeth nipping before his tongue soothed the ache.

If he carried on like that, she might climax just from his mouth on her breasts. As he switched to the other breast, giving it the same attention, she ground harder against him, the wetness from him coating her hand, allowing it to slide faster over his cock.

"Stop." His hand stilled her as he let her nipple go with a pop. "I need to be inside that sweet pussy."

Bram flipped her so she lay on the bed and stood over her, his cock standing proud over his jeans, the rest of him still clothed and it was fucking erotic as hell. Shedding his jacket, he lifted a hand behind his head, pulling his t-shirt off. Now, the beauty of all those tattoos was exposed in the light coming from her bathroom light, the same one she'd left on that morning, and it made her mouth water, wanting to explore them with her tongue, as did the V of muscle at his hips.

Bram smirked at the hot look she was giving him and dropped to his knees on the floor, his shoulders pushing her legs apart. With large, capable hands he undid the button on her jeans and pulled them and the cream lace G-string down her legs. She was on the run, but nice underwear was a must for her, and the one thing she wouldn't give up unless she had no choice.

"So fucking sexy."

His head dipped and he didn't ease in or tease. Bram went straight for the kill, his tongue licking up the seam of her pussy, lapping at her like she was his favourite treat before suckling on her clit and making her whimper, her fingers grabbing hold of his hair and holding on tight.

"Don't stop."

"Never."

Bram pushed a finger into her pussy. Not used to the intrusion her body clamped down and he growled as he fucked her with his finger before adding another and doing some kind of twist action which made her scream as her climax hit her from nowhere, making her arch off the bed.

Bram withdrew his fingers, a sexy smirk gracing his handsome face as he crawled up her body, kissing her hips and belly as he did. Aoife curled her legs around him, bringing him closer to her body as he slid his cock through her lips, rubbing her sensitive clit, making them both groan.

"Condom."

He kissed her and she could taste herself on him and, instead of turning her off, it turned her on to taste herself on his tongue.

"Be right back and leave the bra on. I like looking at your tits like that, imaging my cock sliding through them."

Dirty talk had never been her thing until now, and now she couldn't get enough of his dirty words.

She watched, her brain scrambled of any thought except the man in front of her rocking her world. He grabbed a condom from his jeans and stepped out of them, showcasing the ink on his groin and legs. Seeing him sheath his thick cock as he rolled the latex down the length made her clench her legs together to ease the ache that was building again.

"You wet, Irish?" Aoife stayed silent as he prowled towards her, his fingers finding her pussy and sliding through the wetness there. "Fucking soaked for me."

Instead of getting between her legs like she'd expected, he moved up the bed beside her and sat with his back to the headboard. Holding out his hand, he pulled her up to him and kissed her.

"I want you to ride me, darlin'."

Aoife grinned and straddled his hips, her heat rubbing against his cock as she lifted up. Grasping the base of his dick, she slid down, slowly, his huge cock filling her, stretching her and she threw her head back as she bottomed out with him inside her. It had been so long for her that it took a second to get used to the feel of him inside her. Bram gripped her hips, seeming to fight the urge to move and giving her back the control he seemed to instinctively know she needed.

Her heavy eyes came back to his and he held her tight, his hands squeezing and stroking as he looked at her like she was a feast and he was starving to death. She clenched around him, bringing his eyes back to her face.

"Where the hell did you come from?"

Aoife didn't answer but began to ride him, slow at first as she got used to his size. Finding her rhythm, she sped up slightly, letting instinct take over. His mouth was on her nipples, suckling hard, flicking the tight buds as his hands tilted her hips and he hit that special place inside her that made her cry out in pleasure.

As her second orgasm built, her movements became jerky and Bram took over, fucking into her from beneath as he chased his climax too.

"One more for me, Irish. I need to feel that tight pussy squeeze me as you ride me."

His words and the sensual assault he was laying on her tipped her over the edge and she sobbed out his name as waves of pleasure drowned her. Seconds later, Bram came and she could feel the heat of his seed inside her as it sparked off a ripple of pleasure inside her again.

His head landed on her shoulder as he pulled her closer, holding her to his body and she liked how it made her feel safe.

"I think you fucked me dry."

Aoife laughed. "I highly doubt that."

Bram looked at her from under lashes that should be illegal for a man. "You're incredible. Please say we can do that again?"

"It was fun, but I'm not looking for anything serious. My life is a mess right now." She wished things were different, that she was the woman he'd met tonight. The truth was she wasn't the confident sex goddess that had come from nowhere, igniting the best sex of her life.

"I understand, but maybe I can stay for a bit longer and get my strength back and we can have the rest of the night?"

Something about the boyish charm and the way he made her feel protected, even if it was a fallacy, called to her. Aoife wanted that more than anything, hell she wanted more with this man who she knew in her heart was special. He was honest and kind despite his bad boy looks and filthy mouth.

"Let's have tonight and make it one to remember then."

Bram rolled her to her back and kissed her as she felt his length harden against her thigh.

Aoife pulled away with wide eyes. "Already?"

"What can I say, you inspire me."

Aoife shook her head, laughing and feeling free knowing that tomorrow she'd have to make plans to leave this place and these people and this sexy man just to stay alive. Regret, sharp and painful, made her chest ache.

"Kiss me, Bram."

So, he did, and she didn't think of her future or the hell she faced if her father found her. She enjoyed every second of her night with Bram, knowing it would be a memory she'd need to keep her sustained for years.

CHAPTER 6

Bram sucked in the cool fresh air, expanding his lungs and taking in the sight before him. Looking out onto the vista of green hills and the forest covered in frost gave him a sense of home he hadn't thought to have in this place. Looking behind him at the castle where he'd grown up, it was hard to connect that boy with the man he was now.

Hundreds of years of history was buried in those walls. He'd grown up on the stories of his ancestors, of the wars with the English, and seen the cannonball still buried in the south wall as a reminder of the battles they'd survived.

Ten years and only a handful of visits back home, one to see his parents buried after the car crash that had killed them, his sister's wedding, and the kid's christenings. Regret was a useless emotion, but it was hard not to wish he'd made the effort to see his family more.

Seeing his mum and dad, when they came to visit him wherever he was based, he'd seen the sadness in their eyes, and he wished he could have made them proud instead of becoming the black sheep who had tarnished the name.

"There you are. I wondered where you'd gone."

Bram twisted to see his sister waddling down the stone steps and rushed to her, taking her arm. "You shouldn't be out in the cold."

Lana gave him what he called her 'mum' look. "Nonsense, I walk these grounds all the time and know every crack in the stones."

Bram still worried when he was there. "I know that, but it's icy this morning and I worry about you."

Lana kissed his cheek. "I know you do, and I love you for it, but there's no need. I have enough with Rory fussing like an old woman, I don't need my brother doing it too. These boots are sturdy and at this stage, I'd probably roll."

He glanced down at her walking boots then back to her belly. "True, you're as round as you are tall these days."

Lana slapped his arm. "Rude."

"Just kidding, sis, and you know whales are my favourite fish."

"Dick."

Bram laughed, feeling freer than he had in months. Being with Lana and her family and seeing how well she was doing always made him happy. He just wished he could find the same peace she had. Something had changed in him of late and he didn't know if it was his parents dying, or just that he was at an age where he would've been thinking about a family had his life gone in a different direction, but something was off. His thoughts skimmed to Irish and the night they'd spent together on Friday.

The sex had been off the charts, he'd never felt a connection like that before, but it was more. He liked talking to her and if the sex hadn't been on the table, he'd still have wanted to spend time with her. He'd had to force himself to leave early for his trip up here or he knew he would've ended up back at the pub, fawning over a woman who he knew could puncture a hole the size of a freight train in his emotional armour.

He and Lana walked the grounds of the herb garden before heading back inside where Mrs Murrel had tea and cake waiting for them.

She'd been with their family since before he was born and he could see she moved slower now, but as Lana said, she was family and she had a job here as long as she wanted it.

Her small, arthritic hand cupped his cheek as he bent slightly so she could reach. "Och, it does my heart good to see ya, lad."

"You look as beautiful as ever, Mrs M."

"Ah, get on with ya silver tongue. I'm an old woman, but I sure do love hearing your voice in these halls again."

"It's good to be back, Mrs M." He was surprised how much he meant those words.

"Well, I best get on. I promised the wee ones some of my million-aire shortcakes for after school."

"You spoil them, Mrs Murrel," Lana gently scolded.

"Aye, maybe I do, but they're good kids and I enjoy doing it and they never forget their manners, so it can't be all bad."

"That's true. I guess Rory and I are doing something right."

"You're wonderful parents, and don't you forget it."

Bram watched Mrs Murrel bustle out and was glad Lana still had her here as a mother figure. "So where is Rory?"

His brother-in-law was a brute of a man, tall, with wide shoulders and a bright shock of red hair and a large, bushy beard. He looked like he could fell a tree with one swipe of his axe and was the reigning champion at the caber toss. But with Lana he was like a gentle puppy and adored the ground she walked on, and she adored him. Rory was the man he would've picked for his sister. They'd met at the University of St Andrews and clicked immediately and never looked back.

"He's out sorting a poaching issue north of the lakes."

Bram tensed, poachers were an issue with people hunting out of season and on the property without permission. It was a frequent problem because they could fetch a hefty sum for out of season meat. It was also dangerous as these people were often criminals not worried about hurting innocents.

"They're going after the stags?"

Lana nodded and shifted around, trying to find a comfortable position. "Yes, and wild birds. We've also had reports of night hunting."

"Let me know if you need me to do anything."

Lana nodded and sipped her tea. "I will, but I'm sure Rory will handle it."

Bram had little doubt he would. The man was more than capable, and he loved this estate as much as Lana did. Between them they'd taken it from just turning a profit to bringing in a huge income every year.

Using the money his parents had left them when they died, they'd revamped the rooms using a top London designer and now rented the main house out for weddings, corporate events, parties, they'd even had it used on the set of a new Netflix series. Lana and Rory were a formidable team and did it all while raising their four, soon to be five, kids.

"When's the next event?"

"We have a wedding next week, which is why I want this done. I can move everything we keep into storage and that frees up these quarters for guests wishing to stay here."

Lana and Rory had renovated one of the cottages on the huge estate, so it now resembled a large modern home. It gave them space to be away from the goings-on at the main castle and the chance for the children to be normal kids. The room they were now sitting in was their parents' quarters in the castle. They'd kept them after the estate was revamped, stuck in their ways, and used to living a certain way. They'd made it work, but now they were gone.

"We should probably stop putting this off then."

"I guess." Lana stood and stretched, her hand rubbing her belly. She was a good mother, and he adored her kids. He couldn't see that for himself, not with how he lived, and he liked his life for the most part. He was happy being fun Uncle Bram and somewhat resigned to that being his lot.

He followed as she led him into their father's study, the smell of cigar smoke like a punch in the gut. His father was everywhere in this room, from the smells of leather and smoke to the decanter of whisky on the silver tray. His desk was antique Edwardian mahogany, with a green tooled leather top.

"Do you want to start with the desk and I'll go through the filing cabinets?"

"Yeah, sure."

Bram sat at his father's desk as he had so many times as a child, pretending he was his dad and drawing or scribbling nonsense. Later this had been the place he'd always sneak to when he wanted peace. His dad would often sit on the old chesterfield by the fire reading a book and drinking a whisky as he did, his silent presence a comfort and a spur to do the best he could to make his dad proud.

"I miss him, you know."

Lana looked up at Bram's surprising words and he was as shocked as she seemed to be by the admission.

"He loved you so much, Bram. They both did and they missed you all the time."

He rested his elbows on the desk, his thoughts a whirl of emotion as memories assailed him. "I know I should've come home more but after what happened I was so angry, and I knew I'd disappointed him."

Lana moved closer, resting on the edge of the desk, her eyes on his face full of sympathy and love.

"How can you forgive me for what I did?"

Lana frowned. "Forgive you? What the heck are you talking about?"

"If I had just let you stay in the same pub as me, you would never have... he..." Bram couldn't get the words out, they stuck in his throat like a shard of broken glass.

"Ray Walsh raped me, Bram, and nobody was to blame except him. Certainly not you and after years of counselling, I know not me, either. It took me a long time to come to terms with what happened and to be able to look at myself in the mirror and not see someone who was dirty and spoiled but I got there."

She reached out and touched his shoulder and he shuddered, his grief and pain almost overwhelming as he listened to his sister tell of how she'd conquered her demons. He was a trained soldier, a killer, and yet it was his sister who was the strong one, the true hero. Getting shot at didn't make him a hero. Overcoming adversity and pain, learning to heal and move on, to live the life you want despite what you've gone through, that was a true hero to him.

"I'm just so angry Dad wouldn't let you report it."

Lana shook her head. "What? Dad wanted me to report it. He called the police and everything, but I refused to talk to them. We both know his family are loaded and even at eighteen, I knew they'd tear me apart on the stand trying to prove his innocence. I just couldn't bear to go through that. I wanted to forget, to crawl into a hole and forget his name."

Lana sucked in a huge breath. "When I heard he was dead, I felt so guilty. I worried your life would be over and that it was my fault. Dad said he'd fix it and the next thing I knew, you'd joined the army. He was so proud of you. He kept every letter you wrote, had pictures of you in your uniform by his bed."

Bram pressed his lips together, a slight grimace creasing his features as a sigh escaped him. His belly knotted and he felt a dull ache in his chest which he tried to rub away with his hand. "All this time I blamed him. Thought he was the one that stopped you going to the police, that I had shamed the family name."

"No, never. He was so proud of you and the man you became." Lana chuckled low. "It was pretty annoying actually."

Bram smiled but it was lame at best, his thoughts too jumbled for anything real. "I think this will take some time to process."

"I know, but remember your family loves you. We all did, even mum who was away with the fairies on pain meds most of the time."

Their mother had suffered a broken hip after a riding accident when he was six and had never fully recovered, relying on strong pain killers for her to function. They had become an addiction that his father had allowed because he loved her and hated her to see her cry.

Bram wondered now if the man he'd seen as his father was who he really was or if he'd projected his own self-worth onto a man who loved him for who he was.

Lana stepped away and returned a minute later with an envelope, passing it to him. He saw his name in his father's handwriting. "What's this?"

"Dad said to give it to you when he died. I meant to send it and forgot. Baby brain."

Bram turned it over in his hands but knew he couldn't read it, not yet, not when his emotions were so fragile. "Thanks." He tucked the letter in his jacket pocket. "Now, let's get this done. I want to come with you to collect the kids from school."

They got the rest of the paperwork squared away and he spent a lovely week with his sister and her family. They walked, talked about their childhood, remembered the good times, and she and Rory brought him up to speed on everything to do with the estate. He'd assured them they didn't need to run anything past him and that as far as he was concerned, the estate was theirs to run. If he had his way, he'd pass the title to Lana but if he refused it, it would move to his male cousin who was a dickhead. So, he kept the title and always stayed out of the public eye.

He still received a yearly dividend which he put straight into savings for his nieces and nephews. He didn't need the money and it was their parents who worked their asses off every day for it and he was, after all, non-existent to the outside world. He was a shadow.

Lying in bed on his last night in his sister's home he knew the trip had been good for him. He'd laid some ghosts to rest, uncovered some truths which should've been done earlier but were now out in the open.

Maybe now he could let his past go like Lana had done and make a life for himself that didn't involve just killing. He loved his job, and what he did, that dark side of him needing an outlet, and being allowed to right wrongs that normal channels couldn't gave him peace. He just wanted more, someone to share it with. Seeing Rory and Lana together he knew he wanted that. The way they could communicate without words, the closeness, as if it was them against the world.

He hadn't heard from Bás all week and hadn't expected to. He'd needed a break and it had done him good. The policy was when you left Shadow for vacation time, because of the intensity of the work, they wouldn't call you in unless it was imperative to the safety of the team. He'd enjoyed his time away, but he was eager to get back to work now.

His thoughts turned to the mysterious Irish girl with the incredible body who'd rocked his world. She'd been on his mind all week and now he couldn't wait to get back to see her.

CHAPTER 7

AOIFE FLUFFED HER HAIR ONE MORE TIME, WONDERING WHY SHE WAS bothering when she hadn't seen hide nor hair of Bram all week. She'd told him it was a one-time thing because she knew she couldn't offer more and would be gone soon, plus she needed to concentrate on staying alive. Yet deep down where only a tiny part of her still believed in good, she'd wished for more, that he might be the one to sweep her off her feet and free her from her life. It was a stupid childish thought and one she couldn't afford. The only person she could rely on was herself. Moving forward, she'd even decided to cut Peyton from her life. It would only lead to pain for her friend, and she didn't deserve that.

As she walked the now familiar path toward the pub, she laughed humourlessly at herself. She'd been silly to get her hopes up even for a second. It was a luxury she couldn't afford and got her nowhere in life except disappointed. To expect Bram to be some kind of knight in shining armour was ridiculous. He was a good guy and, in another life, maybe they would've had something, but her life wasn't a fairy tale.

The air was cool, a light fog hanging over the small valley at the base of the mountains where the town was situated. Sometimes the fog didn't burn off at all and lingered all day and into the night, giving the land a mysterious quality that reminded her of home. Dublin was a beautiful city, but it was the time she'd spent with her mam and grandma in Avoca, near County Wicklow that had been the best times of her life. Perhaps that was why she felt such an affinity for this place, it reminded her of happier times.

Even though it was only eleven in the morning, she was already tired from not sleeping. Watching her every move and tensing at every sound or voice was exhausting her, both mentally and physically. This was the furthest she'd got away from her family even though it hadn't been the only time she'd tried to run. The last attempt had been two years ago, and she'd paid for that with a broken femur, two cracked ribs, and a cracked tooth. That hadn't been the worst though. No, that had been watching the guard that let her slip away being tortured in front of her and then his life slowly ebbing out of him onto the cold, concrete floor of the cellar.

They'd almost broken her will that time. She'd been so close to giving up and ending her life, only her mother's last words to her had saved her. She'd wanted Aoife to be free, to flee her gilded cage before it was too late. As she walked the curving road, she stopped at the sound of a vehicle, her heart racing fast, fear paralysing as she waited for the car to come around the corner. Every second was filled with worry they'd found her until she saw Mrs Jones, who waved, her face barely visible over the steering wheel of the Land Rover she drove. The relief almost brought her to her knees and with it the realisation that she had to leave. It was only a matter of time before they found her, they always did.

She'd already waited too long in the hope she'd get to see Bram one more time and it was a mistake. No man was worth dying over, not even one who fucked like he did and could make her laugh and feel safe. Safety was an illusion, afforded to the blissfully ignorant and she hadn't been that for ten years.

It was Friday, which meant they'd be busy tonight with regulars letting their hair down as much as they could in this small village. It always shocked her how much these farmers could drink and still get up at four am the next day to tend to the farm. As Mr Johnson told her, farming was twenty-four-seven for three-hundred and sixty-five days a year. Nobody got a day off, or a holiday in farming. It also meant tips would be good. She'd take tonight, leave first thing, and head deeper into north Wales.

With her mind made up, Aoife quickened her step to the pub. Walking in through the back door, she called Bob's name and heard nothing. He was most likely in the cellar fixing the barrels. Stowing her bag, she took off her jacket and headed into the bar to get things ready to open up.

Aoife stopped dead at the sight of broken bottles, smashed glasses, chairs turned over, tables destroyed, and the mirror behind the bar cracked and hanging from the wall in front of her. The place had been trashed. Terror gripped her by the throat so tight she fought to get air into her lungs. She went lightheaded, pins and needles shooting through her body as she realised they'd found her.

A groan from the other end of the bar broke the spell of fear and she ran toward the sound. She found Bob on the floor, his face a mask of blood and bruises, his top half propped up against the bar, his legs in front of him. He lifted a weak hand as she ran to him and dropped to her knees.

"Oh my god, Bob." Her hand didn't know where to touch so as not to injure him more as it shook with anger and fear. "This is all my fault."

"Help me up."

"No, you need to stay there. I'm calling an ambulance."

"No, don't do that, girl. I'm okay. Just some cuts and bruises. Now help me up onto that chair."

Aoife hesitated for a split second before doing as he'd asked, hitching her shoulder under his armpit and taking as much of his weight as she could to help him stand. He groaned and she knew his injuries were way worse than he was letting on to her.

Rushing behind the bar, the glass crunching under her boots, she grabbed a clean towel and wrapped some ice, then grabbed a glass and poured a brandy for Bob.

"Here, put this on your cheek, it should help with the swelling. This is for the pain." She handed him the glass, which he tipped straight back without question then gently held the ice to his face. "I'm so sorry, Bob." Tears clouded her vision as she tried to blink them away, guilt making her look away as the pain of it clogged her throat.

He looked at her through the eye that was still open, and she wanted to sob at the sympathy she saw there. "They are bad people, girly. You need to leave, now."

Hurt by his words but knowing she deserved his rejection she nodded and began to stand. Bob grabbed her arm, and it was a firm grip for an old guy. "I ain't blaming ya, sweetheart, but I don't want them getting their disgusting hands on an angel like you. I want you to call this number." He motioned for her to get a pen and he jotted it down on a beer mat with a shaky hand. "I know you don't want to take help from anyone, and I know you're scared, but you can't fight this alone forever and I don't want to hear of a sweet thing like you ending up on a slab because of them monsters."

Aoife was crying now, tears flowing down her cheeks unchecked. Even after everything that had happened to him, he was still trying to help her.

"Now, come on, don't cry. It'll be alright, you'll see." Bob's one arm came around her and she wished again her own father was like this man and not an evil bastard.

"It's my father. He's the one looking for me." She didn't know why she confessed that to Bob, but she did.

"Bastard don't deserve you. Now, promise me you'll call this number as soon as you get home."

Aoife didn't know what to do or who to trust, but she was running out of options. They were here, and they clearly knew she

59

was too. What choice did she have? She trusted Bob to steer her right, although he had no idea what she was up against. "I promise."

"Good. Now, go. You don't have much time."

"I can't leave you!"

"Course you can. Just hand me the phone first and I'll have Donald Winters come over and give me a hand to clean up."

Aoife swallowed a choked sob and took the mat from his hand. She went to get the phone, grabbing her bag and jacket at the same time. Dropping to her haunches, she kissed Bob on the cheek. "I'm so sorry, Bob."

"Just promise you'll call the number."

Aoife nodded. "I promise."

With that she raced for the door, looking out to see if she could see anyone before she ran towards the village where her home was. Every step was filled with fear as she waited for the heavy hands of her father's guards to land on her shoulders, but they didn't come. Finally, she reached the safety of her home and checked all the small safety measures she'd put in place, like the clear tape on the door jamb and the smudge of lip gloss on the door handle which proved nobody had touched her door.

Rushing upstairs she began throwing her meagre possessions into her bag, not stopping to fold, just sweeping it all in leaving drawers open as she went. Finding the brand-new burner phone she'd stashed in the floorboards, she opened it and slipped in the sim card before she sent a quick message to Peyton telling her what had happened.

Knowing she had to be more careful than ever, she used a code they'd worked out years ago. Then she took out the mat Bob had given her and looked at the number with hesitation. These people might be able to help, or they might not, and she was risking their lives by getting them involved, but she had no other choice. She was at the end of her rope.

Dialling the number, she waited as it rang twice, her eyes on the locked door she knew wouldn't keep anyone out who really wanted to hurt her.

"Hello, VRE Insurance limited. What is your policy number, please?"

Aoife pulled the phone away and checked the number she'd dialled again finding it correct she put it back to her ear. "Hi, I was given this number by a friend who said you might be able to help me."

"What is the name of the friend?"

"Bob Harris. He said you could help me."

"What kind of insurance policy are you looking for? Car or home?"

Aoife shook her head, frustration making her eyes water as her crossed leg bounced against the bed. "I don't need insurance I need help."

"I think you have the wrong number."

The line went dead, and Aoife fell forward, her hands covering her face in utter despair as the will to keep fighting started to ebb from her. Maybe she should give up and go back, take the punishment she knew was coming.

The phone rang in her hand, and she jumped, jostling it to the floor. She grabbed for it and stared at the unknown number before she answered. "Yes?"

"Listen carefully, I need you to go to the back of the property you're in and climb down the back window. Move quickly and silently as you're about to get company at the front door. Run to the edge of the field and keep low as you run east along the hedgerow. When you get to the wooden stile, someone will meet you there."

"Who are you?"

"A friend of Bob's. Now, go."

The woman cut the line dead and immediately she could hear banging on the front door.

"Come on now, princess, come out. Don't make my men come in looking for you, there's a good girl."

Hearing her father's voice so close almost made her pass out from fear, but the memory of what he'd done to Bob and so many others before him made her steel her spine. They wouldn't be hurt in vain for her to give up at the last hour.

Doing what the woman had said, she opened her window and shimmied down the drain, landing as softly as she could as sounds from the front of the shop drowned out her landing. Running as fast as she could, keeping her head low, and not looking back, she made it to the field and followed the hedge line east.

Blocking the yelling behind her from her mind, she kept going, her focus on getting to the stile. As she neared, she glanced around, seeing nobody waiting, and wondered if she'd taken a wrong turn. Just as she got close, she was grabbed from behind, and a cloth bag thrown over her head. Before she got the chance to scream, a hand was placed around her neck and darkness followed.

CHAPTER 8

Waking suddenly in an unfamiliar room, Aoife began to panic, sitting up fast, her legs falling over the side of the bed. Touching the back of her neck, she found no pain but knew she'd been knocked out somehow, even though her mind was clear of any residual drug-induced side effects. Perhaps they'd given her something new, a drug that her father or his associates had invented to make them more money. A sealed bottle of water sat beside the single bed, and she took it, taking a small sip as she tried to figure out what had happened. She didn't recognise this as one of her father's places, but she knew he had safe houses scattered throughout England and Wales and she had no clue how long she'd been out.

Her legs were a little wobbly as she stood, testing her legs to see if they'd hold and if she could make a run for it if the chance arose. She twisted to inspect the room, which was a clinical white with a dark grey tile floor, but it wasn't cold and as she crouched to the ground, she felt the heat from the floor and realised it was heated from underneath. A packet of biscuits sat on the small dresser and her bag lay on the ground beside it. Her confusion increased as to where she was and she wondered if perhaps it wasn't her father but someone else that had snatched her from that field.

Relief flooded her at the sight of her things. Everything was there except the burner phones. It was silly to feel so much for her belongings but they were all she had in the world now and it gave her hope, small as it was.

"You're awake."

Aoife turned, almost stumbling over her own feet as a huge man she didn't know reached out to steady her. Aoife snatched her hand back, backing away from the giant who put his hands up in supplication before taking a step back.

"Where am I?"

"Safe."

Aoife cocked her head. "That isn't an answer." Cursing inwardly at her quick tongue and stupidity for sassing this man who was smirking at her, she stepped back again putting more distance between them. He could literally snap her like a twig if he chose to and she couldn't do anything about it.

"We're friends of Bob's."

Concern for the kindly man who'd shown her nothing but compassion and support filled her chest. "Is he okay?"

The handsome black man folded his arms across his huge chest, nodding. "He's going to be just fine."

Aoife sagged to the bed behind her, relief taking her legs from her and making tears prick at her eyes. "Thank God."

"He's a tough old bastard."

Aoife tried for a smile knowing it came off as more of a grimace. "What's your name?"

"They call me Hurricane."

Aoife looked closer at the man who was still standing just inside the door as if aware she might be afraid of him, and it was that which eased her anxiety a little. He had skin like polished ebony over muscles which she was sure could bench press a small car. His high cheekbones would make models weep and full lips that her friends had paid a fortune in silicone for. "Well, Hurricane, what's the plan?"

"I came to see if you wanted some food. I can't take you out of this room until the boss approves the job, but we can make sure you're fed and safe."

She would've objected but right now she was as safe as she'd felt in forever, and as exhausted and hungry as she was from the emotional trauma of this morning, she'd take it. There'd be time for demanding answers when she felt stronger, and food and rest would give her time to formulate an escape. Aoife was a lot of things, but a fool wasn't one of them. She couldn't fight her way past this man if she wanted to on a good day. Her best bet was to rest, eat, and see what they had to say and pray they'd help her.

"Food would be good, thank you."

"Any special dietary requirements like allergies or whatever?"

"No, nothing. I'm not really a fussy eater either."

Hurricane grinned, showing straight white teeth and crinkles at the corner of his eyes. "Be back shortly. There's a bathroom through that door and fresh clothes if you want to change."

Hurricane pointed to a door she hadn't noticed and then closed her door before leaving. She didn't miss the way it locked though and wondered if he was keeping her in or others out.

Deciding to explore the small bedroom and bathroom, Aoife found a shower and fully equipped bathroom suite with towels, toiletries, and clean clothes with the tags still on in a cupboard.

Taking the quickest of showers, she washed her hair, enjoying the warm water for a second before rinsing the shampoo out. Brushing it through with a brush, she used one of the hair elastics to hoist the heavy mane into a ponytail. Putting on the brand-new white cotton underwear and bra set, she pulled on clean, skinny black jeans and a dark navy jumper.

Walking back out to the bedroom, she stopped short when she saw a petite platinum blonde woman placing a tray down near the bed. She glanced up and bright blue eyes peered back at her from dark lashes.

"Oh, hi. I brought you some shepherd's pie with a side of broccoli and green beans. There's also some chocolate cake if you want it afterwards."

Aoife glanced at the tray, her stomach rumbling loudly and making the young woman laugh.

"Sorry, I forgot breakfast."

"No problem. I'm Snow. It's nice to meet you."

"Aoife. So, are you all named after a weather event?"

Snow laughed, her body in constant motion as she bounced from one foot to the next as if she couldn't keep still. "No, mine is because of my hair and pale skin. They tease me I could blend into the snow."

"Ah."

"Anyway, eat it while it's hot and I'll be back to take you up to meet the boss in a couple of hours. There's a book in the corner if you want to read."

Aoife noticed the book that hadn't been there before on the bed and smiled as she recognised the well-known romance author, Freya Barker. "Thank you."

As the door closed, the click of the lock engaged, and Aoife took the tray before sitting on the bed and tucking into the food. It was delicious, full of flavour and comfort, just like her mum made and she didn't feel the tiniest amount of guilt as she wolfed down the chocolate cake either. She needed every ounce of energy she could get. It was divine, and homemade if she wasn't mistaken.

Laying back on the bed, her wet hair dangling off the side, she thought about that morning and the last week. She should've run after the warning from Peyton, but she'd been a fool, wanting to stay where she felt safe for a just a bit longer. Sleeping with Bram had made her even more careless. She foolishly wanted more even though she'd been the one to say it was impossible. But the chemistry between them was unlike anything she'd felt before and it wasn't just the mind-blowing sex. Talking to him was like talking with a friend. It was easy, comfortable, he was funny and made her laugh but with a little fizzle in her belly from the sexual tension.

She must have dozed because she woke when the door opened, and Snow stepped into the room.

"You ready to meet the boss?"

Aoife rubbed her eyes, wishing she had the armour of make-up to hide behind, but she only had her grit and her backbone, and she hoped it was enough to convince these people to help her. "As ready as I'll ever be."

Aoife followed Snow out the door and into a large corridor that was as clinical and nondescript as the rest, past closed doors, the low light on the walls giving nothing away.

"There will be a few others in the room as we make a lot of our decisions as a team but don't be afraid or intimated. They're good people on the inside—at least mostly."

Aoife swallowed, trying to find her earlier confidence again at Snow's words. What the hell did 'mostly' mean? Were these people criminals or some shady government organisation that were helping so she'd help them in return for taking her father down?

"Don't panic, Aoife. If you get scared, just imagine them with no clothes on. It works for me when I'm nervous."

Aoife couldn't imagine Snow being scared of anything, she seemed small but mighty in every sense of the word. However, at this point, she'd take all the advice she could. Snow stopped at a door and knocked. It swung in and she walked through, motioning for Aoife to follow and then she didn't have to imagine the man before her naked because she'd seen every glorious inch a week ago.

His sexy lips curled up into a smirk and he sat his ass against the edge of the table. "Irish, good to see you."

"Bram?"

"One and the same, sweetheart."

CHAPTER 9

Bein barely had time to dump his bag on his bed and stow the unopened letter his father had left him before a message came through from Bás to meet him in the conference room in ten minutes. Thank God he'd slept on the flight or he'd be shagged out from travelling all the way from his home in the Highlands to Hereford.

He knew he shouldn't, and he'd agreed to one night, but after thinking about Irish all week he knew the first chance he got he was heading to the pub to see her. Hands in his pockets as he headed toward the conference room and feeling more refreshed, he was ready to catch up on what had been going on here while he was gone.

He opened the door and saw Lotus sitting beside Hurricane at the round table. Snow was sitting next to Titan, with Bás in his usual chair at the head of the room near the coffee pot.

"Welcome back, dickhead," Lotus called, and he gave her the middle finger salute making her grin.

He laughed taking a seat beside Titan. "You know you missed me."

"I didn't but Titan did. He took your place in the ring."

Bram side-eyed Titan with a wince at seeing his face. "Sorry, man."

"It's fine, but you owe me a beer."

"What a coincidence, I'm heading there shortly."

Bás held up his hand to halt the chatter and the room instantly went silent. They'd had a laugh but when Bás used a certain tone everyone knew it was time to work. "Nobody is going anywhere."

"What's going on, boss?"

"We had a call around midday today from the number we gave Bob for emergencies. It was from the barmaid at the pub. She said she was in trouble and needed help. We went through the normal process and called her back. Lotus and Hurricane were already in town and when they got to the scene, men were at her front door."

Bram felt his gut tighten, a knot of anxiety making him feel nauseous. "Is she okay?"

"Yes, we picked her up and brought her here. Bob wasn't so lucky. He suffered a broken cheek, four broken ribs, and is going to be black and blue for a while."

"Fucking bastards! Do we know who did this?"

Bás shook his head. "No, but I had Watchdog run facial recognition and the girl going by the name Debbie is actually Aoife Doyle. She's the only daughter of the Irish mafia boss, Jimmy Doyle."

It all made sense now, the accent, the fake name, the awareness, and the fear. Doyle had a reputation as a mean son-of-a-bitch, who'd sell his own grandmother if it got him a deal.

Titan was pursing his lips, his association with gangs putting him on the radar with a few mob bosses. "Doyle is volatile and ruthless. He won't stop until he has her back."

"He isn't fucking getting her back," Bram stated hotly, bringing the focus to him.

"Something you'd like to share, Bein?"

He glared at Bás not wanting to tell him he'd slept with her but knowing honesty was the most prized commodity in this team and

MADDIE WADE

the one thing Bás wouldn't tolerate was lying or withholding information. "I slept with her."

Bás drummed his fingers lightly on the table. "I see. Well, in that case, you won't be involved in the vote to decide if we take this job on or not."

Bram wanted to argue but knew it would do no good. When Bás made a decision there was no talking him around. He was a determined fucker, which was why he was such a good leader.

"Fine." He'd have to pray his team decided in his favour because he knew no matter what if they decided to walk away, he wouldn't be. Irish had been terrified from the very beginning and a person didn't get that way without a very good reason, and they certainly didn't run from the mob without a damn good reason or a death wish, family or not.

"Snow, would you go and bring our guest in, and we can hear her story before we decide."

Snow was up and out the door, clicking it closed softly behind her. She was so light on her feet; it was what made her the best jewel thief in the world, or more accurately, the best retired jewel thief in the world.

"Who brought Aoife in?" He was still getting used to the name on his tongue and it brought forward thoughts of what else he wanted to taste on his tongue, namely her sweet pussy.

"Titan and Snow, while Hurricane and Lotus kept the men busy and made sure they left town."

"Was Doyle with them or was it just his men?"

"He was there and mad as hell when we showed up. We let him into the room and showed him it was empty. We know Bob had said she'd been gone a week when they beat him, so we went with the same story. Said the girl had run out a week ago and asked where we could find her as she still owed rent."

"He buy it?"

Lotus shrugged. "Hard to say with a man like that. He doesn't trust anyone so probably not, but he left, and we shadowed him until he made it to Worcester."

A knock on the door had him standing quickly and swinging it open, eager to lay eyes on the woman who'd haunted his dreams all week.

He felt his lips curl into a smile at the sight of her, wet hair in a ponytail, face scrubbed clean, she was a knockout without a hint of make-up. A natural beauty who didn't need any adornments to be the most stunning woman in the room. Her black denim jeans hugged her curves like a second skin and the dark blue jumper moulded her curves like a lover's hands. Fuck, he was getting aroused just looking at her, so he crossed his arms and leaned against the table to hide his obvious desire.

"Irish, good to see you."

"Bram?"

"One and the same, sweetheart."

Her shock was tempered with the flush of pleasure seeing him brought and made him think maybe his attraction and regret over it only being one night hadn't been one-sided.

Bás stood. "Ms Doyle, please take a seat. My name is Bás, I run this team."

Aoife looked around before taking a seat next to where he'd been sitting. Bram sat down beside her and angled his body toward her, feeling a primal need to protect her or claim her in some way.

"You know my name?"

"Yes, Ms Doyle, we do but we don't know why you need our help, so if you could kindly explain it, we'd be grateful."

Aoife looked around her again and he could see she was over-whelmed by everything and fighting not to show it at any cost. She was wearing another mask, just like the one at the bar and he didn't like it. He wanted to see the Aoife who'd left scratch marks all down his back.

"Okay. Well, I'm the daughter of Jimmy Doyle who's the leader of the Irish mafia. Six months ago, I ran away for the fifth time, and I'll die before I let him take me home."

Bram saw the truth in her words and wanted to kill Jimmy Doyle with his bare hands for making her feel that way.

Bás leaned back in his chair, his hands resting on the arms. "Tell us why you ran away."

"My father isn't a good man, and he's a terrible father. When I was sixteen, he killed my first boyfriend because he found out we'd had sex. He beat me and put me in the cellar of our home where he'd sometimes torture his enemies and made me listen. I ran away not long after that and he found me the same day. To teach me a lesson he let his men take turns raping me. He said if I was already sullied what did it matter to him."

Bram thought he might puke at hearing her words, his chest tightened, the hair on his arms standing on end at the calm way she relayed the information. The similarities between her and Lana were minimal but the shame he saw on both of their faces was the same, as was the wall of detachment. What made it worse was the matter-of-fact way she spoke of it, as if it happened to someone else.

"Go on."

Bram glared at Bás who ignored him.

"This time he promised my hand in marriage to Igor Popov."

Lotus leaned forward. "The leader of the Russian mob in Miami?"

Aoife nodded at her. "Yes."

"Jesus, he makes your dad look like the father of the year."

"I know. I'd heard the stories and I tried to refuse but my father wouldn't hear of it. He wanted the alliance to strengthen his ties with the Russians and help his export of drugs into the US."

"So, you ran." Bram itched to reach out and take her hand, but he knew he couldn't. They were a hook-up, not a couple, and now she was meant to be a job, but he knew deep down she was so much more than that. He had all these feelings swirling around inside him that he didn't understand, but one thing was for sure, he wasn't walking away until he understood them all.

"Yes, I ran. Peyton, a friend of mine, helped me get away."

Lotus had her pen poised as she was making notes. "Peyton what?"

"Peyton Lawson. She's a PTSD councillor. We met at school."

Bram glanced at Lotus wondering if it was a coincidence that Aoife ended up here after all. He was pretty sure Peyton was the same person who'd helped his friend Smithy when he was suffering from severe PTSD caused by hurting the woman he loved while he was drugged. Lotus knew him well, and it was a complicated relationship they shared as she'd been on the side of the woman who'd drugged him.

"And Peyton helped you get away and make your way here?"

"Yes, I used codeine and cyclobenzaprine to drug the guards."

"What were you using those for?"

"I had a broken femur a few years ago and I still get pain sometimes, so the doctor prescribed it."

Lotus cocked an eyebrow. "How did you manage to drug them?"

"I had free roam around the inside of the house, so I put it into their morning coffee. I knew my father would be out at his club overseeing his takings from the night before and then I ran. I honestly can't believe I made it this far without him finding me, but I won't go back."

Bram fought his smile as pride in her resilience to overcome, and he fought the instinct to reach for her hand. Although he didn't care how it looked to his team, he knew she would care. Aoife was doing everything she could to show strength, even though he knew it was costing her and every person in the room knew it too. He wouldn't make her feel weak or exposed by giving in to his own needs.

"Well, Miss Doyle, we need to discuss this and decide what we're going to do. Bein will walk you back to your room and we'll let you know shortly."

"What happens if you decide not to help me?"

"Then you'll be driven to a location, given the bare essentials, and we'll wish you well in your endeavours."

Aoife gulped and nodded. "Okay, thank you."

Standing, he held the door for Aoife before giving his team a look he hoped conveyed how much he wanted them to take this case. It wasn't a usual case for them, but it wasn't unheard of either. Lotus gave a short chin tilt, and he knew he had her support, and he'd need it because either way he was going up against the Irish mafia.

CHAPTER 10

"So, I guess you do a little more than mountain rescue?" Aoife walked beside Bram towards the room she'd not long left. She had to admit seeing him had been a shock, but on reflection maybe not. He'd been giving off that alpha protector vibe all along and although she didn't really understand what he did here or what any of them did, she knew they helped people.

Bram chuckled as he held her door open for her to enter. "Yeah, and your name isn't Debbie either, so I guess we both told a white lie."

Aoife looked at the floor, not meeting his eyes and he could see she hadn't liked lying to him. "It's fine, Aoife, I get why you did. Running from a monster like that takes guts and smarts and changing your name was a smart thing to do."

"Not enough though. It's never enough."

Bram stopped her just outside her room, his hand reaching for her arm and holding on, the small touch wasn't enough but he knew it would have to be. She was a job, and he couldn't cross that line with her now. "You did great, Aoife, you got away and you stayed ahead enough to stay alive. Let us do the rest now. We know how to deal with men like him."

Aoife lifted her head, her eyes twinkling a little now, with his reassurance. "You're kind of a badass then?"

Bram chuckled. "I guess you could say that."

She stepped inside the room, sexual tension filling it as he glanced at the bed, making the room feel smaller as he followed, leaving the door open to the hallway so he wouldn't be tempted to do something he shouldn't.

Aoife paced, rubbing her hands against her jeans

"Do I make you nervous, Aoife?"

She shook her head in vehement denial despite the fact he could practically hear her heart as it banged against her chest. "No."

Bram stepped forward lifting his hand to her face. Her eyes closing, she leaned closer in an indication she wanted his touch as much as he wanted to touch her, but he couldn't. Everything was different now she was a case to them and as much as he wanted to, he'd keep his distance so he could do his job. Instead, he merely tucked a strand of hair back from her face, his fingers grazing her skin and making goosebumps break out all over his body at the shudder that ran through her.

He tried to hide his pleasure at her reaction but failed, the smirk on his face telling her that he knew exactly how he affected her, which was a jerk move. Turning her back on him, Aoife fussed with the drawers before turning back to find him waiting with his hands in his pockets. Stillness was a skill he'd learned at a very young age. To wait out in the cold for a stag or doe to appear was a lesson in patience but waiting for a target to come into focus behind his sniper rifle was a skill only honed by practice.

"Do you think they'll vote to take the case?"

So that was what she was worried about. She didn't know these people, not even him really, although he felt like he knew her. He knew if anyone could help her it would be them.

"I hope so, but even if they don't, I won't let you fight this alone,

Irish." He'd already made that decision but he knew it was the right one as soon as he saw the relief ease her tense shoulders.

"What do you mean?"

Bram moved closer and sat on the edge of the bed and she sat beside him. "I'm not going to just let them send you away to fend for yourself against that animal you call a father."

Aoife shook her head. "I don't understand."

"If they vote not to help you, then I'll help you alone."

Aoife stood before moving back, taking away the temptation she represented to him. "No, you don't know what you're taking on. My father is evil. I won't have you going up against him alone."

Bram stood abruptly, anger tightening his jaw. "Wait, let me get this straight. I can't go up against him without my team, but you can?"

"That's different, I'm his daughter. This is my fight."

He didn't understand her stubborn refusal and it was making him crazy. Bram moved closer grabbing her hand in his as tears hit the top of her cheeks before sliding down her face. "I can handle your father, Irish. Please, if the need arises, let me do this for you."

Aoife looked up at him through watery eyes. "Why?"

"Because it's all I can give you and I need to."

He could see in her eyes that Aoife knew what he was saying, what had happened between them had no future. Despite the insane chemistry and sex they'd shared, whatever this was between them was temporary if not already over. She looked as sad about it as he was, and regret pooled in his belly like day-old Chinese takeaway.

"You don't owe me anything, Bram. We hooked up. It was great but neither of us made promises to each other."

"Maybe not, but you're more than a hook-up, Aoife. You're a good person who deserves a life without terror in it and I can give you that, so let me, please."

A sigh escaped him when she nodded her head in acceptance.

"Good girl." Because he couldn't help himself, he pulled her bowed head into his chest and kissed her hair, just holding her for a minute and relishing every second.

"Knock, knock."

Aoife moved to jump back from Bram as Snow stepped in, but he stayed her with his hand on her hip. A slow smile creased Snow's pretty face as she looked between them, jumping to exactly the wrong conclusion.

"Sorry to interrupt, but Bás wants to see you both in the conference room."

"We'll be there in a second," Bram answered for them both and Snow grinned before she skipped off out the door.

"Is she always so happy?"

"Yeah, pretty much, but don't let her fool you. Snow is deadly and cunning in a way I've never seen before."

"Who are you people?"

"I'd tell you but then I'd have to kill you."

Seeing her expression Bram chuckled and gripped her hand pulling her from the room. He told himself it was an innocent touch or friendship to comfort her nerves, but the truth was he didn't want to let go of her now, maybe not ever, but he knew he had no choice. "Don't panic, Irish. Snow likes you so you're safe."

"Yay." Aoife gave a half-hearted wave of her free hand, making him laugh harder.

Bram let go of her hand before entering the room. In here he was Bein, not Bram, and saw Bás, Snow, Titan, Lotus, and Hurricane waiting for them. He could feel the tension radiating from Aoife as she took a seat between him and Snow as she waited for the answer. What he was willing to do for her was so much more than he should've promised but he didn't regret it. Bás would fight him on it but he'd lose. Bram was determined to do this with or without the team behind him.

CHAPTER 11

"Well?"

"We're going to help you, Aoife, and at the same time put an end to the trouble being caused by Doyle's reign of power."

Relief was so sharp her legs almost gave way and she sagged against Bram's side, letting him hold her tight as the news sunk in.

"Thank you, I can't tell you how much this means to me. I don't have any money at the moment but as soon as I can access my accounts I have a trust fund from my mother that I can use to pay you."

Bás cocked his head. "We don't want your money, Aoife. We just want to know that men like him aren't spreading their filth into the world."

"Are you sure?"

"Positive." He clapped his hands and turned as a stunning woman with long dark brown hair walked into the room followed by two dogs. A German shepherd who was almost entirely black with just a slight tan colour on his chest and another dog who was black and white and looked similar to a sheepdog.

Aoife watched Bás smile, his eyes tracking over the beautiful woman. Before looking back to her, his expression cleared. "This is Valentina. She's our resident dog handler and search and rescue specialist."

Aoife smiled as Valentina leaned in offering her hand, surprising Aoife. "Pleased to meet you."

Aoife was surprised by how normal she seemed, compared with the others. "It's nice to meet you too." Aoife turned her attention to the dogs stepping forward and then stopping as the black and white one growled low. "Who are these two?"

"Beruhigen," Valentina commanded, and the dog instantly stopped growling and seemed to relax. "He thought you were a threat and Monty here is very protective." Valentina looked over at the German shepherd who was watching his master and not her. "Scout here is more chill. You can pet them now."

Aoife, who was a little warier now, approached slowly and let both dogs sniff her hand and before long both were licking her and allowing her to make a fuss of them.

"They're gorgeous."

"They are but Monty is going through his teenage years. He's only two and trying to test the boundaries. Scout is four and knows who the boss is around here and accepts it isn't him."

"You'll see Val in and out of here a lot, she also has rooms here." Bás drew attention back to him.

"You all live here?"

Bram touched her back, making her shiver from the light touch of his hand on her body, and she turned to look at him. "We do, we all have suites that are like apartments."

Bás glanced at Lotus who smirked. "You might as well go over the rest of the rules while you're at it."

Bram ignored them. "You'll have access to the room you were in before, the common rooms, and the gym. All the other rooms are locked and can only be accessed by one of us. If you wish to leave the facility, you'll be escorted out but will be blindfolded to ensure the secrecy of the location. If an alarm goes off, then you'll be locked in whatever room you're in until either one of us comes to get you or the perceived threat is averted."

"Jesus, who are you people?" She'd asked before as a joke. Now she really was wondering just who she'd accepted help from and whether she'd made a deal with the devil, no matter how handsome he may be.

"The people who are going to haul your ass out of the fire." Lotus fired back.

Aoife nodded, holding her tongue. Going up against Lotus was a mistake and she wasn't a fan of confrontation at all. Plus, she was right, Aoife had no right to question them when all they'd done was help her. The woman was waspy with her words though and very defensive, but it was easy to see it was out of loyalty to her friends. "Good enough for me."

"Great, now let's get some more details from you so we can come up with a plan on how we're going to set you free."

Aoife liked Bás. Despite his rough demeanour, she got a good vibe off him, in fact off all of these people, and after living with true evil, she knew her radar was good. It felt like hours as she poured out everything she knew. Telling them everything about how she'd lived, her escape, Peyton, how she'd got there, and her father's business dealings, which were a lot less detailed. As a girl, she hadn't been privy to anything deemed sensitive. Her father believed women were good for two things, making a home and fucking.

It was a sad reality she'd come to terms with very quickly once she'd reached puberty and he'd gone from treating her as his little princess to seeing her as a commodity he could use for his own gain.

"What do we all think?" Bás glanced around the room waiting.

Bram was sitting beside her, a silent comfort in this overwhelming and surreal experience.

Titan sat forward, his huge arms resting on the table. He was a quiet, thoughtful, calm presence in the room. She didn't know his background, but it was hard to see him as violent in any way. He seemed almost zen in his mannerisms. "We need to figure out how he always finds Aoife. From what she says, nobody should've picked up her tail so quickly."

Lotus chewed on the end of a pencil. "We also need to speak with a few of our contacts about his set-up. I can do that."

Bás nodded and an unspoken conversation seemed to take place between them. "Bein, I want you and Titan to go and speak to Bob and find out if we can get a description. Watchdog is going do his magic, and Lotus has the mafia angle sorted."

Bás absently petted Monty, who was seated at his feet between him and Valentina. "Hurricane, I want you to head to Ireland and find out whatever you can from people on the ground. Be discreet and don't push too hard, people like Jimmy will have spies all over the place and will know the second you set foot in his town, so be very careful."

His eyes zeroed in on her and she tried not to shrink back in fear at the intensity in them. She knew she was safe there, but old habits were proving harder to shift than she'd like.

"I need you to turn your phone on and contact Peyton. My team needs to speak with her and find out exactly what she said to Jimmy."

Aoife felt her back go rigid in defence of her friend. "Peyton wouldn't give me up."

"Maybe not but you and I both know with enough incentive anyone can break."

"Not Peyton. She's loyal and she helped me to get away."

"And you always got caught."

Aoife didn't care what this man said, she'd never believe that Peyton had betrayed her. "Fine, I'll call her."

Hurricane pushed her phone across the desk to her, the battery already inside and Aoife lifted it, waking the screen. She glanced at Bram who nodded his encouragement. Hitting dial, she let it ring and ring. "She isn't answering."

"Is that usual?"

"It happens sometimes if she's in a session with a client."

"Bram, go pick up Peyton and take her to Eidolon. Jack has cleared an office for you to use."

"Sure."

"I'm going too."

Bram and Bás shook their heads and Aoife saw red. "I'm not going to be locked up like a fucking prisoner. I didn't escape one jail to replace it with another. I need to see if my friend is okay." She was practically vibrating with anger at being suppressed to the role of victim and 'little woman'. She might be a victim, but she was also a survivor and she wouldn't let anyone, even if their intentions were good, push her into a submissive role again.

"You should let her go. Peyton is more likely to talk if she sees her friend is safe."

Bás seemed to hesitate as if taking on Valentina's words and then capitulated. "Fine. Lotus, you go with them. I want someone watching their back."

Lotus smiled. "Let's go, loser."

Bram shook his head and stood, waiting as she walked ahead of him before catching up to her side. "Lotus and I have to just grab a few things. Can you wait in your room for a few minutes?"

"Yes, of course. I need a minute to get my head around every-thing to be honest."

His hands were in his pockets, and he rocked on his heels, moving close to her before backing out of reach again, the imaginary veil between them already in place. "It will be okay, Aoife. You have us now."

As she watched him walk away, she prayed that she hadn't just signed their death warrants.

CHAPTER 12

HE COULD FEEL THE TENSION COMING OFF AOIFE AS THEY ASCENDED TO THE ground floor level of the building. He was sure being blindfolded was unpleasant, especially given everything she'd been through and, despite sleeping together, they were mostly strangers. Yet keeping the location and entrance to Shadow a secret was imperative for their very survival.

They'd exited through the back, where the vehicles were housed and as they made it into the secure area where the cars, helicopters, and even a small plane were kept, he grabbed the keys for the Range Rover Discovery. It was top of the range but covered in mud, allowing it to blend in with the other farm vehicles in the area.

Helping Aoife inside so she didn't trip, he threw the keys to Lotus and jumped in the back beside Irish, and Lotus gunned the engine.

Ten minutes later he leaned over and released the blindfold. "Sorry about that."

Aoife gave him a small smile and looked to the window, no doubt trying to get her bearings. Lotus took a bend a little fast and Aoife slid into his side, the lap belt doing little to stop her, but as she went to move away, he put a hand out to stop her. He was in unchartered

84

territory with Aoife. She was confident in some ways, the way she'd taken on Bás to make her case for coming with them evidence of that, but in other ways, she still seemed skittish. He'd need to tread carefully and make sure she felt secure.

"What kind of music do you like, Aoife?" Lotus caught his eyes in the rear-view mirror, and he could tell she'd picked up the same vibes and was trying to relax her. Despite her stand-off nature, Lotus was a good person. She should've been called hedgehog because she was sweet on the inside but seriously spikey on the outside.

"Um, pop, chart stuff, I guess. My father didn't like music on in the house growing up, said it polluted the mind."

"She likes Taylor Swift."

Aoife glanced at him, a small smile on her face. "You remembered that?"

"Of course."

"Well, let's have a listen and see if we can find something we like, and I'll try not to hold Taylor Swift against you."

Lotus fiddled with the screen and before long music was blaring through the car as Lotus and Aoife sang along like they'd been friends for years, with Lotus, despite her derision, knowing every word to *Shake it Off*. He smiled to himself and thanked God there wasn't any tequila in the car or fuck knew how this would've ended.

"We need to go out and party when this is all over and you're free. Have a girl's night and let our hair down."

"I'm sure when this is over, I'll be the last person you want to see."

Bram frowned as he angled in his seat to see her expression. "Why is that?"

"Believe me, after the shit I'm going to land at your door, you'll be glad to be rid of me."

"Ack, Irish, you underestimate the shit we're going to bring to Jimmy Doyle's door. By the time we finish with him, he'll be wishing he'd been the perfect parent to you and never had the unfortunate pleasure of meeting us."

"Hooya." Lotus laughed from the front and Aoife's eyes widened. "I'm starting to think you're all a little bit crazy."

Lotus laughed. "I'm insulted. I'm not a little bit anything."

"Alright tone it down a bit, Naz. you're gonna freak Aoife out."

Lotus snorted. "As if seeing your pale ass and limp dick hasn't done that already."

"Oh my God, you two are worse than kids. And for the record, it wasn't limp."

Bram winked at Aoife as he laid his arm around her and kissed her head, breaking all his own rules, but at least he didn't do what he really wanted to do which was kiss her until neither of them could think straight. "Damn straight it wasn't"

"Okay enough foreplay, children, we're almost there."

Sure enough, they were driving through the middle of Hereford, over the new bridge, passing the football ground, and making a turn as they headed back out of town towards the Worcester Road. Lotus indicated and pulled into the drive where Peyton both lived and worked.

Aoife went to jump out, but Bram stopped her, his gaze on Lotus as they both spotted the side gate was open. Maybe nothing but neither were taking a chance. Bram unholstered his handgun from under his jacket and saw Lotus do the same. Aoife looked at them with wide eyes, seeming to sense something was off, and probably more than a little shocked at the sight of the weapons.

"Would that gate normally be open?"

Aoife shook her head. "No, Peyton has a new puppy and she worries about him getting on the road, so she's anal about the gate being shut."

"I need you to stay behind me." Aoife nodded and he was pleased she was following his direction so well. "Good girl."

Lotus exited first, with him moving in behind her. Grabbing Aoife's hand he placed it on his waistband, and she held tight, moving in sync with him. He checked the front windows and found nothing amiss and they slowly, silently moved around the back. The back garden overlooked the Lugg flats which flooded regularly but were a great place for dog walkers and gave a direct escape route onto the main road out of town. At the far end of the garden was a wooden structure which was as large as his flat and was the building she must use for clients. Every part of his body was strung tight, his brain mission-focused, aware, as if every sense was heightened for danger.

Being friends with Smithy, he and Bram had talked about Peyton a few times. From what he knew, he agreed with Aoife about her loyalty. But he wasn't about to take chances with her life.

Lotus nodded to the house, and he frowned, seeing the sliding patio door open. He motioned for Aoife to stay behind him as he and Lotus entered first. Plants and pots were smashed on the floor, and he could hear Aoife's intake of breath at the first signs that all wasn't well there. Lotus headed upstairs and he cleared the ground floor, finding no sign of Peyton or anyone else.

The sound of a dog barking caught his attention as Lotus came down the stairs and he felt Aoife's hand tighten on his belt. Glancing at her, he headed toward the office at the end of the garden, the barking getting louder. He indicated Aoife should wait with Lotus who understood that they could be about to find a dead body and he didn't want Aoife to see that.

Reluctantly she let go of him and he pushed open the door. The room was large and warm with a pale green couch, a coffee table, and a glass desk in the corner. As he stepped inside, a white fur ball attacked his leg, the tiny thing holding on to his trousers with its razor-sharp little teeth. He could shake it off, but he didn't want to hurt the little guy. He kept moving towards the desk, where he could see a woman's foot, dread filling his belly that he was about to find the dead body of his girl's friend.

He gritted his jaw at the first sight of Peyton. She was lying on the floor on her back, black and blue, and covered in so much blood it was hard to make out her features. As he crouched to feel for a pulse he realised she was breathing.

"Lotus, get in here."

He knelt beside the injured woman, trying to find the source of the blood, but it was tricky with so much of it coating her body. She was unconscious, probably from blood loss and pain, but he was glad to find her pulse was strong.

"Peyton."

He heard Aoife scream as she dropped down next to him, her hand reaching for her friend as the furball finally let go and moved to Peyton, licking her face in between licking Aoife's hand.

"We need a medic and fast."

"She needs a hospital," Aoife cried and Bram took her hand in his and pulled her away as Lotus took over Peyton's care.

Her eyes kept darting back to her friend who was injured and bleeding, and he could see the guilt and worry etched on her face.

"She needs an ambulance."

Her tear-filled eyes begged him, but he took her face in his hands and made her look at him. "Listen to me, Irish. If we take her to a hospital, your dad will find you. He'll have men at the emergency department waiting to grab you. Why do you think he left her alive?"

"But she's hurt."

Tears fell down her cheeks and he felt his heart break a little for her pain. He hated seeing her like this, seeing the spark he knew burned inside her so frail. "I know and we're going to get her some help, but we can't go through traditional methods. Peyton is hurt but there aren't knife or bullet wounds."

"But there might be internal bleeding or broken bones. Believe me, my father doesn't hold back."

Bram's jaw tightened, knowing the reasons she knew this was because she'd been on the receiving end so many times. If he ever got in a room with that man, he wouldn't be responsible for his actions. "I know. Do you trust me?"

Aoife nodded without question. "Yes."

"Let me make a call, okay?"

"Okay."

He pushed her gently back to her friend's side and called Bás, who picked up on the first ring. "Peyton is injured. They got to her before we did. My guess is they're waiting to grab Aoife at the hospital."

"Fuck. Okay, I'm going to call Jack and have him send Waggs to your location, or do you want to take her there?"

"We'll take her to him. We're sitting ducks here and I don't like it."

"Fine, I'll let Jack know your ETA."

"Yeah, tell him twenty minutes."

Bram hung up and moved quickly to Peyton who was moaning in pain even though she was still barely conscious.

"We need to move. Grab the car and park it across the gate so I can slide Peyton straight in the back. Waggs is waiting at Eidolon."

Lotus ran off and Aoife bit her thumb nail as he gently eased his arms underneath Peyton's broken body. A whimper of pain made him wince as he transferred her into a fireman's hold, so he had a free hand to hold his gun. Violence against women was one thing he couldn't tolerate, and this fucker was going to pay.

"Aoife, can you grab the furball?"

She nodded and he knew having something to do and concentrate on would keep her from falling apart until he could hold her in his arms and allow her the safety and freedom to do so. She grabbed the dog under the belly and followed him out of the office. As he was halfway across the lawn, the first crack of gunfire hit the ground in front of him.

"Get down." He dropped to the ground, with Peyton in his arms and used his free hand to fire in the direction the shot had come from. Glancing back, he could see Aoife was pinned down in the hedge that ran the left side of the property.

"Lotus, we're under fire from the east side of the property, probably the garage roof." He used the comms in his ear to let her know the direction of the shooter.

"On it." He laid down fire, praying there was only one shooter and hoped Lotus moved her ass.

Less than a minute later he saw a man in a dark suit fall headfirst from the garage roof and land on the stone patio.

"Target down, let's move."

Standing, he went to check on Aoife and found her already on her feet and moving toward him. Satisfied she was okay, he got Peyton to the car and loaded her in the back. Aoife jumped in the front beside Lotus, and they were off, tyres squealing as Lotus got them the hell out of there.

"We need a clean-up crew."

His friend pressed the button on her comms. "On it."

Bram stabilised Peyton as Lotus relayed the need for a clean-up team at the house. Checking Peyton's vitals again and happy she was as good as he could make her, he turned to Aoife to see her looking down at the injured dog in her arms, tears running down her face.

"Aoife, honey, are you hurt?" His hand moved to her and she shook her head.

"No, the bullet hit Bertie." A sob was wrenched from her shaking body as huge, tear-filled eyes came to his.

Shock was setting in and he glanced at Lotus who increased her speed, knowing the need to get her safe was chasing him.

Jack was waiting at the gate when they arrived at Eidolon, the barrier up so they could drive right through. As the vehicle stopped, Waggs came running out with a stretcher, a beautiful woman with dark hair beside him, a white lab coat over her jeans.

"Bein, how is she?" Waggs helped him get Peyton onto the stretcher.

"Vitals seem good, but she took one hell of a beating and I think she has a broken wrist and most likely a few ribs."

"This is Dr Decker. She's a friend and Neurosurgeon, and unfortunately for her, married to Mark."

"Nice to meet you. Let's get her inside and we can assess her injuries."

Bein didn't wait to watch them take care of Peyton, Lotus would do that. His only worry now was Aoife and how damn close she'd come to dying. If she hadn't had Bertie in her arms, the bullet would've torn right through her.

As he approached the car, she was still sitting holding the dog in her arms. Opening the door, he touched her shoulder, so as not to startle her. "Give me Bertie, Irish, I need to get him some help."

"Is he dead?"

"I don't know, sweetheart. Let me take him and we can get Valentina to look at him, you get cleaned up so you can be with Peyton when she comes around."

That seemed to get her to snap out of the fog of grief and shock she was in currently. Once she'd handed him the dog, he cast a glance over her making sure none of the blood was hers. It would be so easy for him to lose his mind right now, the panic seizing him at the thought of anything happening to her.

He didn't know when exactly it had happened but in the two weeks he'd known her she'd become important to him. She'd smashed through the shell around his heart that kept people at a distance and made him care about her.

Seeing no injuries, he let out an unsteady breath and felt the knot in his gut loosen. "Come on, let's get inside."

CHAPTER 13

Bram had hardly left her side since they'd arrived. It had been embarrassing to fall apart in front of strangers but the female doctor who said her name was Savannah had been kind and sweet. Bram had insisted she get checked out and there wasn't a mark on her, which she realised was a minor miracle. A shiver went through her at the thought of how close she'd come to dying. If she hadn't been carrying Bertie, she knew her life would've ended today, but instead he'd saved her life.

A lump stuck in her throat at the thought of the poor puppy who had been so brave defending his master. Peyton would be devastated when she woke and found out he was hurt. Guilt weighed heavily on her. She knew that, without her, none of these things would be happening.

"Hey, how are you doing?" Bram had a clean black t-shirt on now and she was dressed in a pair of women's leggings and an oversized hoodie someone had loaned her.

"I don't know. Guilty, sad, angry, tired. So damn tired. How is Bertie?"

Aoife felt the wall of Bram's arms encase her and breathed in his scent and the lingering smell of gunpowder on his skin. But she felt safe in his arms like she was exactly where she was meant to be. She knew how stupid that was because they barely knew each other. Neither one of them wanted long term and he'd made it clear to her that he couldn't get involved with her now. She was a job. Yet, never in her life had she felt more like she was home than when she was with him.

"Bertie is going to pull through. Val called in some favours and got a friend of hers to operate and he saved him. It was pretty close but the little guy is going to pull through."

"He is?" Shock and wonder filled her eyes with tears and yet the guilt still weighed heavy.

"He's a little dynamo." He dipped his head to look at her. "What?"

It was crazy how well he could read her. "I still feel guilty."

"I understand all of that, Irish, but you can't blame yourself for this. You had no control over what happened and 'what ifs' will tear you apart."

Aoife sniffed the tears back; she was so sick of crying and just wanted her old grit and fight back. It was like being pulled down into a dark abyss that wouldn't let go and he was her only light right now, which was pathetic, bordering on stalkerish. She was beginning to feel like she didn't even know who she was anymore.

"I know but it's hard not to blame yourself when you know that if your actions had been different then maybe the outcome would've been better."

His arms tightened around her, and she felt his lips against her head. "I know that, believe me I do, but you can't live like that. Things may have been different, but it doesn't mean they would've been better. None of us have a crystal ball, nobody can see the future and if we could, the world would be a very different place and not necessarily for the better."

Aoife was about to answer when the doctor and the man they

called Waggs stepped out from inside the medical room where they'd taken Peyton.

Aoife pulled from Bram's hold. "How is she?"

"She has a broken wrist and few broken ribs, but the tests we did, and the portable X-ray machine, showed no internal injuries. We can cast her wrist, or should I say, Savannah can, and then she can go home. But she'll need to be kept an eye on for a few days, as she did sustain a concussion, and of course, the ribs and bruising are going to take some time to heal."

Impotent anger flooded her at the thought of her friend so badly hurt.

"We can look after her. She can't go home as it's too dangerous. We'll take her back with us." Bram didn't elaborate but Waggs nodded.

"Jack wants to see you, Bein, but, Aoife, is it?" She nodded at him. "Peyton is awake and asking for you."

Aoife turned to Bram who winked and nodded at her to go on. "I'll come and find you after I talk to Jack."

She paused outside the door, knowing that when she went inside, she'd have to tell her that Bertie was hurt and see the look of worry and accusation in her friend's eyes and know she'd put it there.

Pushing open the door, she saw Peyton sitting up in bed, a pile of pillows behind her, the white sheet against the medical gown she wore made her look pale beneath the bruising. Seeing each other they both burst into tears, hers of relief and guilt. Aoife rushed forward and took Peyton in her arms as gently as she could, hugging her friend as they both cried through mumbled incoherent words.

A few minutes later, Aoife gently pulled away and surveyed the damage her father and his henchmen had done. "I'm so sorry, Pey." Her friend's face was a mess, hardly a place on her that wasn't black and swollen, her lip split, a cut over her eyebrow, and both her eyes almost closed and black.

"Hey, no, you have nothing to be sorry for. You didn't do this, your father and his animals did."

"But if…"

"No," Peyton held up her hand to silence her. "No, I won't let him do this. You do not get to carry his guilt or shame."

"But Bertie."

Aoife saw her friend's eyes fill with tears, but she blinked them away and blew out a breath. "I know, Waggs told me. But he's a fighter and I know he'll pull through, he has to. He's my protector and friend and I also know that little hero saved you. Savannah told me how close the bullet would've been to your heart if it had hit you. As much as it breaks my heart that he is hurt, I'm glad I still have my best friend with me."

Aoife gripped her hand tight knowing how lucky she was to have this woman in her life. Aoife sat, not knowing how to explain any of what had happened or even if she should. "Bram wants you to come with us."

"That's fine, but how did you end up here? These were the people I was talking about when I said I had friends who could help you."

Aoife let her jaw hang open in surprise at this news. "It's a long story, but the man I worked for at the pub was attacked by my father and he gave me a number and told me to call it for help. I did and the next thing I know I'm in some secret facility and these people are helping me."

Peyton nodded slowly, her teeth nibbling her bottom lip. "I guess that makes sense since it was a friend of this group who suggested I send you to that pub to find work. He probably thought you'd be safe being surrounded by whoever this group is. He must trust them, and Smithy doesn't trust many people."

"I'm just happy he did, or I'd be in hell right now."

"Oh, Aoife, I wish I could've helped before now."

"God, Peyton, you've been the only reason I've kept fighting. I think I would've been dead by now without you."

Peyton gripped her hand in a surprisingly tight hold. "We'll get through this, Aoife. These people will help you."

"You think I'm right to trust them? I have no idea who they are or what they do, except that it's off the books and they're deadly. I've been around killers my whole life, enough to recognise one. All of them, even Bram, are dangerous killers."

"I don't know them, but I know Jack and the men here. If they trust them, then so do I. They're good people and being a killer doesn't necessarily make you evil. It makes you complex and flawed but not bad."

Aoife grinned. "You're going all shrink on me?"

Peyton shrugged and then winced. "Ouch."

The door opened and Bram and the man who'd met them at the gate walked inside. He was hot, with dark hair and gorgeous blue eyes, older than Bram and her but sexy in a way that made women from five to one hundred and five swoon. He was also wearing a wedding ring.

"Peyton, I'm glad to see you awake. How are you feeling?"

"Like I was beaten by three mafia goons."

Bram frowned and Aoife felt him move in closer to her back, his hand resting on her hip and drawing the raised eyebrow of her friend, who she knew would want answers. She wished she had them to give her, but in the space of two weeks they'd gone from strangers to lovers, and now there seemed to be more, but she had no idea how to define it or even if she wanted to.

She and Bram were nothing to each other, so why did it feel like when he was in a room she had to be close to him, and why for a man who was being professional, did he always seem to find a reason to have his hands on her in some way? She didn't mind, hell she wanted it, felt it the same way but it was confusing as hell.

Aoife had no clue if Bram being close to her would jeopardise his job, but she did know she was beginning to care about him and being close to her was bad for people's health. She'd almost lost her only friend today and she didn't know if she could allow her feelings for

Bram to continue. Perhaps pulling back from him and putting this relationship back on a professional footing was best for all of them and if he couldn't, then she'd have to.

"Well, Bram and his friends will take care of that, and they have our full support. If you'd like to stay with Astrid and me while you recover, then you're more than welcome. I've also had a call from Smithy and Lizzie with an offer for you to stay with them."

"That's very sweet, but if it's okay, I'd like to stay close to Aoife for a bit." Peyton looked at Bram and Aoife turned to look up at him.

"Of course. It's already been cleared for you to come back with us."

Jack clapped his hands. "Right, then that's settled. I'll love you and leave you. Astrid and I have a gender reveal scan later today and she's freaking out."

"Ah, congratulations, boss man," Bram said with a grin and shook his hand.

Aoife wondered why he was calling him boss man. Was this man in charge or was Bás? She had no clue, and her head was beginning to pound from all the stress of the day.

"Thanks, I think it might be my hardest assignment yet."

Jack left with a wave and Aoife stood as Bram and Peyton assessed each other. She knew there were doubts about whether or not Peyton had been the leak, but she knew that wasn't the case, she'd always known that. She could also see that her friend was going to be interrogating her the first chance she got about the way she and Bram were so cosy.

"Do you need anything collected from your home before he heads out?"

"Yes, a few clothes and essentials would be good and maybe my laptop? I need to let my clients know I'll be out of commission for a few weeks."

"I can arrange that. We'll need to blindfold you when you get close to our facility. Jack says that won't be a problem for you."

"No, I understand but please tell me you have Wi-Fi and a warm bed where we're going because I need a bed, and a metal foldout isn't going to cut it right now."

Aoife saw Bram smile and noticed he had a dimple in his left cheek, making him look younger and innocent when she knew he was definitely not innocent. Quickly shutting down thoughts of him naked, she looked back to her friend, who was looking peaky now that the pain relief was wearing off a bit.

"That we can do."

"Fine, I'm ready when you are."

"It's going to be an hour or so before we can leave."

Aoife saw her friend stifle a yawn and knew she must be exhausted after everything. Laying a hand on her arm she squeezed gently. "Get some rest. We'll come and get you when it's time to leave."

"Thank you, honey."

"Love you, Pey."

"Love you too, flower."

Aoife backed out of the room with Bram, and he led her toward a kitchen and sat her down in a chair.

"Cuppa?" Bram held up a mug that said, 'Thanks for all the orgasms.'

"Please."

She watched Bram make her tea and bring it and a bowl of sugar over, placing them in front of her. He pulled up a chair so he was sitting closer to her and leaned his elbow on the desk as she stirred in her second sugar. Aoife leaned back slightly to put some distance between them when what she really wanted was to lean into him and let him take the weight for just a little while.

"How did she take it?"

Aoife felt her heart squeeze at his caring concern for her friend. "Waggs had already told her. She was upset but she said Bertie had protected me and she was glad I was okay." She sipped her tea, to push down the tears that threatened to fall.

His hand covered hers, making her want to cry even harder. "Look at me, Irish."

Aoife lifted her head at his command and saw heat and warmth, but more than that she saw determination.

"I know it hurts but you're going to be okay. We're going to fix this so you can have all the things you never dared wish for."

Lotus chose that moment to walk in, her eyes moving over them both. "You need me to get anything from Peyton's place?"

Bram stood, backing away from her. "Yeah, she wants clothes, essentials, which I guess is girly shit, and her laptop."

Lotus arched a brow. "Girly shit?"

Bram waved a hand in the air. "You know, stuff."

"You're a dick."

"Fuck off, Lotus."

Aoife was taken aback by the animosity for a second until Lotus winked at her and she realised that was just how they were. As dysfunctional as the rest of them.

CHAPTER 14

"WHY THE FUCK IS AOIFE IN THE KITCHEN WASHING THE FUCKING FLOOR?" Bram slammed through the door to Bás' office, his temper hanging on by a thread. It had been two days since they'd arrived back after the attack on her friend and Aoife had withdrawn into herself. The confidence he'd seen emerging from her seemed to shrink back in on itself.

He could understand it. She'd been through a lot, more than he cared to think about in case he lost his mind, but he'd thought they'd had something and now she was keeping him at a distance. Putting barriers up and making excuses to avoid him and it fucking stung more than he'd like to admit. Oh, she was friendly and polite, but she pulled away from his touch and made excuses that she was tired or busy to avoid him.

Perhaps she just didn't want more with him, but he didn't think so. He thought it was something else entirely, he just didn't know what. This was why he never got involved with women, they made him crazy. He just didn't know how to navigate the complexities of them, even having a sister had given him no insight into what he should do.

The problem was he liked her. No, he more than liked her, he cared about her. She pulled something free in him that had been locked away for years and, now that it was free, he didn't know how to lock away that yearning for more. Aoife was everything he should avoid, her baggage was enough to sink a fishing trawler and yet he couldn't stop thinking about her soft smile, or her dirty, husky laugh, the way she fit him so perfectly or the silky softness of her skin. It was the reason he was here picking a fight with his boss when he should be working on the information Hurricane had sent through from Ireland.

Bás looked up from his computer and leaned back, crossing his arms, his manner calm but Bram knew he'd pissed him off storming in here like this. "Care to ask that again like a fucking adult, and not a toddler having a tantrum?"

Bram leaned his fists on Bás' desk. "Why the fuck is Aoife washing the kitchen floor like a fucking skivvy?"

Bás stood so he was eye to eye with Bram, neither man backing down. "Firstly, watch your fucking tone with me. Secondly, she asked if she could help out and I told her she didn't need to but if she wanted to, she could see what needed doing around here and chip in with the odd job."

Bram gritted his jaw, his anger still there but under control now. He didn't know what it was about Aoife, but she pushed his buttons in a way nobody ever had before. "You should've told me."

"Why?" Bás challenged.

Bram didn't know how to answer that because the truth was confusing. She felt like his, as if she should be his responsibility, and yet the reality was, she wasn't and never would be his. The life he led wasn't the kind he could offer her. So why did he find himself thinking about how he could make this work long term with her. "She trusts me."

"She trusts Lotus and Snow too."

Bás wasn't backing down and he regretted storming in here and confronting him, looking for a fight with Bás was like a hiding to nothing. "Fine, I like her, and I know that's not healthy in this situation but it's the truth."

"There we go." Bás sat again, his posture relaxed now. "For the record, liking someone is healthy, but don't let your feelings for her cloud your ability to protect her and do your job."

He was about to respond when an alarm started to blare throughout the facility. Bram looked at Bás and both men were on their feet and running toward the war room.

"Find Aoife and get her into her room, then meet me in the tech room."

Bram was running, his feet hitting the tiled floor hard as his heart beat fast, adrenalin pumping through his blood.

"Bram?" Aoife was running down the hallway toward him, fear in her pretty green eyes that he wanted to take time to eradicate but he didn't have it.

He gripped her arm, spinning her around back the way she'd come. "Irish, I need you in your room where it's safe."

"But what's happening?"

"Someone has breached the outer security and we need to handle it." He pushed her inside and went to close the door.

"Bram?"

"Yes?" He saw his harshness pierce her and regretted his tone. He softened his voice. "Yes?"

"Be careful."

Without thinking, he hauled her into his arms for a hard, fast kiss and then released her just as suddenly, a smile on his face.

"Knew you liked me."

The last thing he saw as the door closed was her shaking her head, a smile on her face and he knew he'd eased her fear for a brief moment.

The door clicked shut, the lock engaging, and he turned, his gun drawn as he ran for the tech room. Everyone was huddled around the outside monitors that covered the search and rescue centre and a half-mile radius including the vehicle entrance to the facility.

"What's happening?"

"We got rats."

Titan stepped back so Bram could see, and he saw five men in tactical clothing, poking around the area where the vehicles were kept.

"We have two up near the search and rescue hub too," Snow pointed out.

"Snow, stay here and make sure the facility is secure. Titan, handle the two men at the hub. Bram, Lotus, and I will handle the other five. Keep them alive if you can. We don't want to draw attention to ourselves, and we need to find out what they want and who they are."

Everyone nodded and sprang into action, with him, Bás, and Lotus heading for the armoury with Snow and Titan. Quickly donning tactical vests, masks, and weapons, they headed out into the escape tunnel that would bring them out behind the attackers. Snow and Titan headed in the opposite direction, him to take action at the centre, and Snow to secure the facility.

"Comms on."

As everyone responded to Bás, Bram fell into line behind him with Lotus on the other side. It was as easy as breathing for him, doing this job, feeling this high as gunfire rushed by him. This was who he was, not because he'd been born that way but because the army and Shadow had trained him to be a skilled killer. This was what gave him a buzz that nothing else ever could.

Nearing the exit, they moved into the cold and fog of the mountains. Each one of them knew this terrain like the back of their hand, and they knew to respect it. A light drizzle was falling, making visibility low, which helped them. Moving silently, they crept through the long grass, keeping low.

Bram spotted the five men easily, even as they tried to blend in with the land around them. They weren't professionals, at least not military trained. They were probably effective muscle, but they didn't have the skill of special forces or any other military branch.

Bás made a motion with his hand and Bram nodded, following his lead as Lotus went left and he went right, fanning out and pushing them so they had their backs to the mountain with no place to go.

"I have the hostiles at the front door neutralised," Titan commented down the comms.

Bram wondered if these men were even wearing comms and if so, why had they not realised the others were in trouble. But then Titan was a stealthy bastard for such a big guy.

Bás double-clicked to let them know all was received and stood, revealing his position. "Don't fucking move."

At his words, one of the men swung around firing wildly and Bram took him out with a single headshot. Lotus fired on the other, who was using his AK like he was an extra in a Rambo movie.

That left three against three with them all in a stand-off.

"Hand over the girl and we'll leave."

Bram tensed his hand, tightening on his weapon at the demand in the strong Irish accent. "Don't know what you're talking about but you're trespassing."

"Just give us the girl."

Bram glanced at Lotus and they both knew these men weren't going to surrender. "You're boring me now, asshole. There's no girl here, so why you don't fuck off home?"

He could see the man's finger tighten on the trigger before he looked to his mate who was around the same height as him. If he wasn't mistaken, they were the same men who'd attacked Bob, the description the ex-operator had given them had been detailed and matched these assholes to a tee.

He saw the second they made the choice to die and all three fired, but they were never going to be fast enough, not up against them. Moving fast, they searched the dead men, finding identification on all of them with names and addresses. He wasn't sure how they could be any more stupid.

"Help me get these bodies into the tunnel. I don't want some adventurous rambler having a heart attack on my watch."

Bram followed Bás' order, dragging the bodies inside the underground space for them to deal with when it was dark.

"Watchdog sent up a drone and the area is now clear, but we need to know how the fuck they got so close." Bás was angry and frankly so was he.

"You think we've got a mole?" Lotus asked the question none of them wanted to voice, never one to back away from a confrontation.

"No, I don't. I trust our team implicitly or none of you would be here, but something is up, and I don't fucking like it."

As they made their way back to the main facility, Bram knew what they were thinking and his instincts wanted to defend her. Aoife wouldn't lead her father's men here, not when she was the one in trouble.

"You think it's Aoife, don't you?"

Bás and Lotus stopped dead both turning toward him in the barely lit underground space.

"I didn't say that," Bás answered with caution.

"You didn't have to. I could hear your thoughts from here."

"You have to admit, Bram, it's strange how we've never had issues before and now we have these fuckers practically knocking on our door."

"I know, but it isn't her. She was the one in trouble, for god's sake."

"It wouldn't be the first time a woman has used an elaborate ruse to wheedle her way in, only to stab the person who trusted her in the heart."

Bram knew what Lotus said was right, but his gut angrily rejected the thoughts.

"I know that, but Aoife isn't that person."

"I hope not."

Bram knew what Bás was saying. He'd have no hesitation in putting her down if she turned out to be a threat to his team. Bás was fiercely loyal but he was also happy to make the hard choices to keep his team safe. If Aoife was a threat, Bás would kill her and not think twice about it. In that respect, he was a cold bastard.

"I'm right and I can prove it. Let me take her away. We can go to my family home in Scotland until we have this sorted."

"You're happy to have her around your family? You're that sure she's safe?"

Bram nodded. "Yes."

Bás was silent but the more Bram thought it through the more he felt this was the right thing to do.

"Fine, but you take Snow and Titan with you."

"Okay. What about Hansen?"

"Watchdog still has the protocols in place, and you can resume the hunt for that bastard when this is dealt with."

"Fine."

"Get ready to leave," Bás turned away before turning back. "Oh, but Peyton stays put."

Bram understood; if they were to split them up and one was a leak or a threat then they'd be easier to identify. Now he just had to hope Aoife was on board with this new plan.

CHAPTER 15

THE LAST SIX HOURS HAD BEEN A WHIRLWIND AND SHE WAS STILL TRYING TO catch her breath. After the building had been locked down, Aoife had paced her room, panic filling her chest that somehow her father's men had found her and these people, who she was beginning to care about, would get hurt. Front and centre had been her concern for Bram.

The last two days had been pure torture, trying to stay away from him, denying herself his touch and company, when all she really wanted to do was curl up on his lap and let him hold her, kiss her. As each interaction passed between them, she'd seen the hurt behind the hard mask he wore. The scruff on his chin became thicker, his hair more ruffled as if he was swiping his fingers through it on a regular basis.

Bram arriving thirty minutes after the building had locked down and telling her to pack as they were leaving had spun her head. She tried to get answers from him then, but he seemed het up, an urgency to him that she didn't like or understand. She trusted him though, so she'd done as he'd asked. She'd been the one to pull away from him, not the other way around.

Aoife had come to understand the last few days that the connection they'd shared was stronger than she knew and walking away would be impossible. She liked him, a lot. Not just the fact he was sex on legs and could fuck like a god, but she trusted him. He made her laugh and was easy to talk to. Feelings were beginning to get involved in a way she hadn't anticipated. She knew it was easier to pull away now than get her heart broken again when she lost him. She needed to get out of this mess and find out who she was before getting involved with anyone else. Yet, when the alarm had gone off and he'd kissed her, she'd known her denial was for nothing. The fear she felt that he might die or get hurt was almost paralysing, and it was that which made her see that whatever was happening between them was unstoppable.

Shaking the thoughts of things she couldn't control from her head, Aoife watched the countryside fly past the car. Yet more wild beauty that called to her, mountains and forests, lush trees changing colour from green to the most beautiful deep orange.

Aoife glanced across at Bram, who was driving the Land Rover, the sleeves of his shirt rolled to the elbow, exposing the thick divers watch and the strong fingers. "Are you going to tell me where we're going yet?"

"My place in Scotland."

Aoife felt her eyebrows meet her hairline in surprise. "But why?"

"Your father's men found you and we wanted you far away from him so we can figure out what the hell is going on."

She pondered that for a moment. The thought of running her whole life was exhausting, especially as he kept finding her with such ease. It would be easy to let defeat win, but she was sick and tired of being sad or feeling weak. She wanted to have fun, to enjoy every drop she could squeeze out of life. Fuck Jimmy Doyle and his men, she was done letting him control her; and that's what she was still allowing him to do by turning away from what she wanted.

"Do you recognise these men?"

He passed her his phone, motioning for her to scroll through his phone. As she did, faces of men she'd known for years, who'd been her jailers, came into view. They were clearly dead, and she didn't feel a second of regret over their lives being extinguished. What did that say about her as a person, that she couldn't show any remorse for their deaths?

"I know them. They were my father's guards. Those five, in particular, were tasked with guarding me."

Bram nodded and took his phone back. Silence filled the cab of the car as the night began to draw in, the light of the afternoon fading to twilight and the beauty of the Scottish Highlands high-lighted by the waning sun. They drove through a small village called McCullum, full of quaint shops, a butcher, a bakery, a general store, and a fruit and veg shop. As well as a few clothing stores, a toy shop, and a pharmacy.

"It's beautiful here! Have you had a place here long?"

Bram glanced across at her with a strange smirk on his face that she found charming. "All my life. I grew up here. Went to school in the village before going to high school in Inverness."

"Wow, really? It's beautiful." Aoife was realising that she didn't know much about Bram. Oh, she knew he was great in bed, that he could make her laugh and protect her from danger, but they seemed to have skipped the getting to know you phase and she'd withdrawn without saying why, which was unfair. "Bram?"

"Irish?"

She smiled, loving him calling her that. "I'm sorry I pulled back from you without saying why."

Bram shrugged. "You don't owe me an explanation, Aoife. Your body is yours and if you don't want to share it then, I can take it."

Aoife angled towards him in the huge vehicle. "It's not that, I do want you, but the shooting and how close I came to dying made me realise that I like you."

"I like you, too."

"But we both agreed we don't have the time or inclination to get involved and I didn't want to get hurt. The truth is I like you a lot and

I was scared of losing another person who I'd come to care for because of my father."

Bram flicked the indicator on the car and made a left turn up a narrow track road, with woods bracing the backdrop and sides.

"I think we missed a step when we slept together. Don't get me wrong, it was fucking phenomenal, but we missed getting to know each other and instead put labels and restrictions on things before we even knew each other. I propose we go back and get to know each other and see what happens from there."

Bram pulled around a corner and a huge castle lit up with lights came into view, momentarily stunning her into silence.

"Aoife?"

She shook her head to clear the vision in front of her and help her concentrate on his words. "You'd be willing to do that?"

"Listen, I ain't saying I won't try and get in yer pants but I think we should get to know each other too. I like you and I think we have something that could be special, but the truth is I don't know how it would work. I'd like to try and see where this leads though. No promises or expectations, just plain old dating."

Aoife laughed and nodded, feeling lighter already, free from the threat even though it still existed.

"I like that idea. Although if we're calling it dating maybe we should actually go on a date at some point."

Bram took her hand and kissed her palm as the vehicle slowed in front of the castle. "That's a great idea."

"And I'm not saying we shouldn't sleep together, just maybe slow it down and let it flow."

Bram smiled and then turned to the castle. "We're here."

Aoife ducked her head to look for servants' quarters, but the front door of the castle opened and three children ran out consisting of different ages, ranging from she'd guess around four to eight. The oldest, a boy with red hair, moved down the steps with his two sisters behind him. A tall, beautiful woman with dark hair and a toddler on her hip stood in the doorway, the light from inside silhou-etting her pregnant body as she watched them.

"Hey, Uncle Bram."

Aoife watched stunned as Bram got out of the car and embraced the boy, who blushed with embarrassment despite seemingly being happy to see him. She turned to see two small faces peering at her through the glass of the car before they were both grabbed in Bram's arms as he kissed their cheeks, making them giggle.

"No, Uncle Bram, that tickles."

Aoife couldn't help but smile at the happy familial scene in front of her. Seeing a new facet to the man in front of her made her glad she'd decided to be brave for a change.

Aoife opened the car door, feeling a little disoriented but hearing the giggles and laughter and seeing the smile on Bram's face eased her anxiety.

"Come away, now, girls. Let yer uncle help his lady friend from the car."

Bram opened the door helping Aoife out before grabbing their bags from the boot. "Don't look so scared, they dinnae bite."

"Bram, it's good to have you back, but I have to say I'm surprised it's so soon. I thought you'd be all familied out by now."

They stepped through the huge wooden doors, which must have been built for a giant, to a large entrance hall that would fit the entire pub she worked in on the ground floor. Large stag heads were hung on the walls, with massive tapestries hanging from ceiling to floor. The floor was flagstone tiles, with huge antique rugs covering them, and a vintage table in the centre had a bouquet of heather, thistle, and white roses displayed.

"Aoife, this is my sister Lana, and these are my nieces, Morag, who's six, and Heather is seventy-five."

A giggle escaped the younger girl's mouth as she rushed to Bram and tapped him on the leg making him crouch to her level. "Uncle Bram, I'm four not seventy-five like Mummy."

Aoife stifled a laugh and Bram choked on the chuckle as he looked at his sister who had her eyebrow raised in warning.

"Charming. You carry them for nine months, let them use your bladder as a trampoline, and this is the thanks you get."

Bram straightened back up after ruffling his niece's hair. "This young man is Angus and the little monkey who is hanging off his poor mother is Fergus."

"Everyone, this is my friend, Aoife." Bram slid a hand behind her back in support and as the eyes of everyone in the room come to her, she was glad of it.

"It's lovely to meet you all. Thank you so much for letting me stay with you."

"It's our pleasure. Come, let's get some food inside you, you must be starving." Lana walked away, letting Bram take Fergus, who she noticed had a brace on his foot. "Mrs Murrel was in seventh heaven when she heard you were coming home again so soon and bringing a guest."

Lana led them into a kitchen that smelled of meat, veggies, and spices, making her stomach rumble loudly.

Lana laughed and Aoife could feel herself blushing. "Mrs M is going to love feeding you up, Aoife, and be warned she'll probably be dropping huge hints about weddings and babies before you have the chance to eat breakfast tomorrow so enjoy the peace tonight."

Aoife looked at Bram in question.

"Mrs Murrel is the housekeeper here at the castle and has been with us since we were born. She's more a surrogate grandmother than a housekeeper."

"You own this castle?"

Bram's cheeks went pink a little, which she found endearing and so far away from the protective badass he showed the world, it made her heart skip a beat.

"Yeah, kind of."

"Aye, he's the thirteenth Laird of McCullum, lord and master of all ye see."

Lana was enjoying this if the smile was any indication.

"McCullum? We passed through the village of McCullum... does that mean?"

"Yep, we own the village, it's part of the estate." Lana was no-nonsense and Aoife liked that about her.

"Wow, I had no idea."

Bram frowned. "Why would you, I don't tell people about my title or my life, I can't do my job with that kind of exposure. Plus, I was made for the life I live and Lana and her husband, Rory, run this estate much better than I ever could."

Bram glanced back to his sister who was pushing two heaping bowls of stew towards them.

"Bram would be great at it. The villagers love him but it's not what he wants and we're happy to do it. The kids love it here and I can be around for them and still work, so it's a win, win."

Aoife tucked into the stew as they sat at the butcher block kitchen island, dipping the bread into the thick, flavourful gravy. It looked like the kitchen had been completely refitted with new appliances, but it still had things like an original bread oven and an Aga, as well as a sleek range. "This place is amazing, and I'd give my right arm to be able to cook like this."

Lana giggled. "Yep, Mrs M is going to love you."

When they'd finished eating and Lana had left for the evening, herding her tired children to the home they had on the edge of the estate, Aoife felt herself fighting a yawn.

"Come on, let me show you your room."

Bram picked up her bags and she followed him down endless hallways before they ascended a wide set of stairs.

"This place is huge, I bet it has some stories to tell."

"Oh, hundreds. Robert the Bruce stayed here in 1305 before he became King. His family were friends with the McCullums, and it was said it was here that he planned John Comyn's murder."

"Well, I have no clue who the second guy is but even I know who Robert the Bruce was." Aoife looked around the old building, almost feeling the ghosts of the people who walked these halls so many years before her. "You can feel the history here, it's almost reverent."

"I know, I always felt it as a kid too. The history, the stories, it's something I never took for granted but I also think it's why I never wanted the pressure of carrying this legacy to the next generation." Bram stopped outside a door and looked down at her, before lifting his thumb to swipe across her bottom lip. "This is you."

Aoife felt her heart skip a beat at his touch, her eyes closing waiting for a kiss that, when it came, landed softly on her cheek. Dragging her eyes open, she found Bram watching her intently.

"You're so beautiful. I want you to know I hear you, Aoife. I can take it slow, but don't think for one second I don't want you."

With that he opened the door, revealing a magnificent room done out in blues and creams. A roaring open fire was going in the grate, and a huge cream and blue rug covered the wooden floors. A four-poster, Queen Anne bed with a blue quilt covered in white flowers was piled high with cushions. A hand-quilted throw had been placed at the foot of the bed, and heavy, velvet brocade curtains hung at the windows.

"The room looks out over the back of the estate gardens. You have a bathroom through there," Bram pointed toward a door beside the fire. "My room is next door, so if you need anything, just shout."

Aoife didn't want him to leave but asking him to stay after everything she'd said was wrong. "Bram, are you sure we're safe here? That it's safe for your family?"

Bram moved close to her, his body almost flush with her own and she felt her heart kick up a beat at his proximity. "Snow and Titan are set up in one of the cottages along the perimeter of the castle and nobody knows we're here but my team."

She hadn't noticed the car behind them until they'd wanted her to in the rear-view mirror, and once again she realised just how good these people were, but would it be enough?

"I know but he always finds me, and I'd never forgive myself if something happened to your family because of me."

"Nothing is going to happen, Aoife, trust me."

"I do trust you."

Bram angled his head to the side, his blue eyes on her, the fire-light flickering behind him. "But?"

"But I know my father."

Bram's jaw tensed in anger. "Your father never met me before. I promise you, Aoife, I'll keep you safe or die trying."

Never in her life had anyone given her such a vow, let alone a man she'd only known a few weeks. Yet the pull between them was undeniable and she believed him when he said he'd protect her. "Thank you, Bram. I don't know how I'll ever repay you for what you're doing for me."

"No thanks needed. Now, get some rest. Breakfast is at eight and you can bet your ass Mrs M will be all over you. After breakfast, I thought I'd show you the estate if you want to see it."

"That sounds perfect."

Bram leaned and kissed her cheek, making her breath catch in her throat at the contact, butterflies going crazy against her insides.

As she got ready for bed, brushing her teeth in the gorgeous antique style bathroom, Aoife tried to push down her fear over the man who had given her life. She decided she'd do her best to live in the now and soak up every second of her experience with Bram in this amazing castle. If she didn't, what was the point of being free?

CHAPTER 16

SMUGGLERS REST PUBLIC HOUSE-DUBLIN

THE GLASS SHATTERED, BLACK LIQUID RAN DOWN THE WALL AS JIMMY DOYLE spun on the man who was nervously fidgeting on the other side of his desk. The sight of the pint of Guinness dripping down the wall, made him wish it was this little pissant's blood and brain instead.

"Tell me again."

The man was in his early twenties, a scrotum he'd dragged from the streets, given a home and purpose too, and here he was disappointing him again.

"Donny the snatch reported back that your men never came down off the mountains. He saw them go up and when they never radioed in like they were supposed to, he went looking but they'd vanished."

"What about the landlord at the pub? Have Donny speak to him and tell him not to be as kind as I was last time." That fucking old man had put up a good fight, even managing to land a punch or two before his men had held him down and beaten him, and still, the old bastard had insisted on lying about where Aoife was.

"We thought of that, Jimmy, but we can't get near. The place is always full, the locals seem to have closed ranks."

Jimmy stood, his hand going to his gun, and pulling it from his jacket. He loved how the little shit paled at the sight. Let him be scared, they should all fucking fear him. Moving around his desk, and standing in front of Mickie the quick, he could feel terror radiating from him, taste it even and it fuelled his high better than any drug, better than any whore on her knees.

This was true power, and he lived for it, was good at it. His men didn't work for him because he was a good boss, they worked for him because he made them rich. They were loyal because they knew if they fucked up, he'd not only kill them, but he'd kill everyone they loved too.

Placing the barrel of the gun against Mickie's head, he released the safety, relishing the way the man shook, not knowing if he'd walk out of there alive or not. "Don't give me fucking excuses. I want my fucking daughter back where she belongs and if I don't get it, then I'll kill every fucking person I meet until I find her."

"Yes, Jimmy."

"Now fuck off before I splatter that wall with your pathetic little brain."

Jimmy opened the office door, letting Mickie scuttle out like the cockroach he was and surveyed the bar area. Spotting Conlan O'Neill, he lifted his chin and the man ambled over.

"Boss?"

"Close the door."

Jimmy took his seat behind his desk, as his right-hand man waited for his instructions. Conlan had been with him since the start. He knew Jimmy better than anyone, his secrets, his weaknesses, and he knew Conlan's. "My men are dead."

"I told you, she has help this time."

Jimmy bristled at his friend's tone, his jaw flexing as he tried to keep his temper from erupting. "I want to know who the fuck they are so I can kill every fucking one of them. I want their faces known to every man we have on our payroll. I want to know what these fuckers had for breakfast and want them all to fucking die."

Conlan nodded.

"Where are we with Popov?"

"He's getting impatient. He's threatening to pull the deal if we don't produce Aoife within the next week."

Jimmy began to breathe through his nose as his anger rose. How dare that fucking Russian dictate to him. He had a good mind to kill the fucker, but he needed this deal to secure his drug routes into the US. He also had a good little sideline in human trafficking, which Jimmy was happy to get involved with.

Now his fucking slut of a daughter was trying to ruin everything for him. After everything he'd given her. A beautiful home, designer clothes, parties, holidays, that ungrateful bitch had fucked him over one too many times.

He'd thought teaching her lesson after lesson with his men and then letting them have their fun with her would break her spirit, would show her how good she'd had it, but she was as bad as her ungrateful bitch of a mother.

His pa had been right when he said women were only good to suck cock and fuck. Allowing a woman the right to choose was a recipe for disaster and look where it had got him.

"What about the tracking chip?"

Conlan shrugged. "Not picking up, but you know after the last time you taught her a lesson the chip was damaged, so the signal is spotty. I have someone monitoring it twenty-four-seven. As soon as it comes online, we'll find her."

"Good, reach out to all of our associates across the country and even as far as Europe. There's a hundred grand reward for information on her whereabouts."

"That will certainly help, Jim."

"Now bring that thieving little prick Aiden O'Malley over to the house and put him in the cellar. I want to have some fun later and torturing that asshole will do."

"Anything else, Jimmy?"

"Yes, did the Italians come through on that heroin shipment?"

"No, nothing yet."

"Then bomb their warehouse at the docks. They don't play by the rules, they pay the price. Nobody fucks with Jimmy Doyle and lives."

"Sure thing, boss."

Jimmy nodded. "Oh, and Conlan, I left you a little gift in your basement. A sweet little thing too. Very much your type and flavour."

He saw his friend's eyes glaze over with lust and excitement and wondered how he allowed his appetites to control him in such a way. Kids weren't his thing, but Conlan was loyal to him and feeding his addiction helped keep him under control.

"Thanks, boss."

He was practically salivating now, and Jimmy knew that his friend would be satisfying his twisted needs by midnight.

"My pleasure, Conlan. You know I look after my friends. Make sure you do everything I asked for first, though. We wouldn't want your wife finding out about your little hobby, would we?"

"Course not. We'll find her, Jimmy. I'll have every person we know on the lookout."

Jimmy sat back in his chair and thought of Aoife. She'd been a good child, quiet and sweet and he'd thought she'd serve him well. Become the golden goose and do her duty but she was a spoiled bitch.

If it wasn't for the deal he'd made with Popov, he'd have her killed. She was nothing but a disappointment. Even his most trusted men had said that in the end, she'd been lame and frigid. Yet, she could whore her body for other men, let them take her virginity and cost him thousands in the process.

If this deal fell through, he'd break her, and then he'd lock her in the dungeon for the rest of her natural-born life. She'd see what making a fool of him brought her and rue the day she'd run from him.

A knock on his door an hour later had him calling to come in. His guard on the door poked his head in. "Jake the scrounch wants a word boss."

"Send him in."

Jake was older, a street rat, who'd washed out of the army, years ago. His head was fucked but Jimmy knew he kept an eye on the streets and missed nothing. In return, Jimmy kept him in fags and booze. "Jake?"

"Jimmy, I thought you might like to know I seen a guy hangin' around. He's been asking questions about you."

"Has he now? What does he look like?"

"Big, black, about thirty, the size of a house, and definitely military trained."

"Where did you see him last?"

"He went into the Mill Motel about an hour ago."

"Thank you, Jake, this has been very helpful."

Jake took his usual booze and fags and left. It was a shame, if he'd been half trainable Jimmy would've liked him in his employ proper, but he knew his head was too fucked to be of use. But with his own men dead, or at least he presumed they were dead, he needed more bodies. Perhaps it had been time for a new guard though and maybe these assholes, whoever they were, had done him a favour and cleaned out the rubbish for him.

Jimmy made a call getting someone to head for the Mill and pick up the nosy parker so they could have a chat.

Maybe this day was looking up.

CHAPTER 17

He'd hardly slept a wink last night, knowing Aoife was on the other side of the wall and he couldn't touch her. It was like a living, breathing need, the urge to have his hands on her in the smallest of ways, and not just sexually. Although thoughts of her in bed had made sleep so uncomfortable that in the end, he'd had to get up and take care of himself so he could get some relief.

Now it was seven am and he'd already been for a run around the grounds and was headed to check in with Snow and Titan. The air was cold and fresh, a bite to it that he loved invigorating his body and mind in a way nothing else could.

"Hey." He walked through the door of the cottage where his friends were set up and found Titan frying bacon, with Snow sitting at the kitchen table with her laptop open in front of her.

"Morning, my Laird."

Since telling them of his title so they weren't shocked by it when they came here, Titan and Snow had been taking the piss constantly.

"Peasants, how are you this fine morning?"

He took a seat opposite Snow as she grinned at him. Titan plated up the bacon and eggs, raising an eyebrow to offer him some. Bram declined, knowing Mrs Murrel would've cooked enough to feed an army.

"Any chatter?"

"No, nothing. Doyle is quiet. I think taking out his top men has wounded him, so he'll probably pull back and retreat to lick his wounds for a bit before coming back at her. Hurricane says there's no movement from his usual haunts and Bás wants him back here. It's too dangerous for him being there alone and we're stretched too thin. You know he hates us being divided like this."

"That's a good call. Has Watchdog found anything we can use?"

"Plenty of rumours, stories that would turn you grey, but nothing we can use."

"I think the Russians are our best way in and so does Bás. Lotus has gone to meet with Rykov."

Rykov Anatolievich was the head of the Anatolievich family and a rising star in the Russian Bratva. He was also a Shadow asset and had a major soft spot for Lotus.

"Do you think he'll help us against his own men?"

Snow shrugged. "No clue, but if anyone can persuade him, it's Lotus."

Bein agreed, she was their best bet right now.

"Doyle won't give up, though, Bein, you know that."

"I do, which is why he has to die."

Titan sat down at the table, a mountain of food in front of him and tucked in, eating half of it before he spoke. "You sure that's a road you want to go down?"

Bein wasn't sure what he meant by that. "What do you mean?"

"Killing for the job is one thing, killing for another person is different, especially when it's revenge."

"This is a job."

Titan arched a brow. "Is it?"

Bein was getting impatient now. "Just spit it out, Titan."

"Listen, all I'm saying is revenge is a path that leads to nothing but destruction. If you want this guy dead because the world will be a better place because of it then go for it, but I saw your face when Aoife told us what her father let those men do to her and you looked ready to commit murder."

Bein banged the table with his fist, making the cutlery rattle. "His own fucking daughter, man. He let them rape and hurt her and he didn't care. A man like that doesn't deserve to breathe."

"I agree, Bein, but just make sure you go into this with open eyes."

"You think I should let him live?"

"No, I don't but I made peace with who I am a long time ago."

Bein relaxed, knowing his team were with him no matter what. "You're a good man, Titan. Support a shit football team but you're okay."

Titan pushed his empty plate away and put his hand over his heart. "Please, everyone knows Arsenal are the best team."

"Yeah, remind me again what you've won recently?"

"Okay, enough boy talk. Can we please discuss the plans for the day?" Snow had been quiet, always slow to get into her energiser bunny routine, but a bundle of energy when she did.

"I'm going to show Aoife the estate and then afterwards see if she wants to go into the village and have a look around."

"Cool. So, are we in the background or what?"

"Well, I'm pretty sure neither of you are going to blend in very well in the village so you might as well come with us."

"Are you saying your people have never seen a brother before?"

Bein laughed at the way Titan called them his people. "No, I'm not saying that but we don't get a huge number of visitors this time of year and any newcomers will be spotted a mile out, which is why I came here. It's like your own private battalion of security for free."

Bram stood, stealing a piece of bacon from Snow's plate, earning him a slap. "Animal."

"You weren't eating it."

"I was saving it."

"Fine, come over to the main castle in an hour and Mrs M can feed you a second breakfast."

"For real?"

Bram laughed at the way Snow's eyes lit up. That woman could eat more than anyone he knew and she still stayed the size of a waif. "For real."

"You're forgiven."

"See you guys in a bit."

Bram jogged back to the castle, rushing through the door and up the wide stairs two at a time heading for his room. Once he was showered and dressed, he tapped on Aoife's bedroom door.

He held his breath listening as she moved around before the door swung open and she was standing there smiling at him, her hair still damp on the ends where it was trying to escape from the bun she'd forced it into. This woman with her wide green eyes and a smile that could outshine the sun, took his breath away. He didn't know what it was about her but every second he was with her he was falling harder and harder, and he didn't want to stop. He hadn't lied when he'd said he had nothing to offer her, but he found himself wanting to be the best version of himself around her.

"Hey!"

"Morning, gorgeous. You ready for breakfast?"

"I am, I got the best night's sleep."

Bram shoved his hands in his pockets to keep from reaching for her, but she linked her arm through his as they walked down the stairs. "That's great. It can sometimes be a bit overwhelming for people."

"It is, but it also has a nice, cosy feel to it, which I know is crazy to say about a place this size."

"No, I get it. I've always felt the same way."

Walking into the dining room, Bram tried to hide the smile from his face when he saw Mrs Murrel had gone all-out for breakfast. The sideboard was loaded down with fruit, fresh bread, croissants, homemade jam, and honey from the estate, as well as cold meats and yoghurt, also made on the estate.

"Wow, look at all this. Are we expecting company?"

"Only Titan and Snow and perhaps Lana and Rory when they get back from the school run."

"That's a lot of food, it looks delicious."

"Och, will you look at the two of you."

Bram spun at the sound of Mrs Murrel. "Mrs M."

"Bram, darlin', 'tis so good to have you back so soon, and with a pretty lady to boot."

He hugged the smaller woman, as she kissed his cheek and then turned to Aoife who was beside him. "Mrs M, this is a friend of mine, Aoife. Aoife, this is the true backbone of the McCullum estate, Mrs Murrel."

"It's a pleasure to meet you, Mrs Murrel, Bram has told me so much about you, and your stew from last night was divine, thank you."

Mrs M patted her hair in pleasure at the praise. "Well, my dear, Bram has been tight-lipped about you. Maybe we can have a chat later and I can give you the recipe for my stew. The secret ingredient is pickled walnuts, you know."

"I'd love that."

"Now, I must get on. Do you want your eggs poached or scrambled?"

"Poached, please."

"Excellent, I'll bring in some toast and bacon shortly and get the eggs going. Coffee is in the carafe and fresh juice is in the jug."

Bram pulled out a chair for Aoife beside his at the end of the table, leaving the two at the head for Lana and Rory.

"Do you always eat like this when you come home?"

Bram chuckled. "God, no. I'd have to live in the gym if I did. Mrs M is taking great pleasure in cooking for more than just Lana, Rory, and the kids and is going way over the top."

"Did I hear my name?"

Rory walked into the room, the huge burly Scot smiling as he held hands with Lana.

"Rory, good to see you."

"Aye, you too. Nice to meet ya, Aoife. Sorry I wasn't here last night but I had to have a call with this producer in the US about exporting our beef."

"It's fine, I don't expect you to run around after us. I'm just grateful you're happy to have us here." Bein knew the man was risking his family's privacy bringing in a stranger this way.

"Yes, thank you, it's very kind of you." Aoife nodded beside him.

"Away wit' yeh. This here is Bram's birthright. We're just taking care of it in case the lad does nae produce bairns."

"What he said was he's happy we're here." Bram took in Aoife's confused expression and explained. Rory's accent was strong and for those not used to it, could prove tricky sometimes.

"Aye, that's right. Now, is there anything we can do to help ya out with this here problem?"

Rory was a big guy and protective of his family, and Bram bringing Aoife there made her family to them. He hadn't known it at the time but the more time he was here the more he realised he'd brought her home for a reason. He just wasn't entirely sure what that was yet.

"I've told them everything. I couldn't lie when it's their children that live here."

Aoife nodded slowly as if embarrassed. "It's fine, I understand and thank you. I'm sorry I brought this to your door."

"Never apologise for something that isn't your fault." Lana was firm as she spoke, but Bram could hear the gentleness in her voice too. Lana reached for Rory's hand, and he took it, giving it a squeeze. "Don't let anyone dim your spirit because of who they are."

"I guess it's become so ingrained in me that I do it out of habit, now." Aoife looked at him, and he touched her leg letting her know he understood.

"Now, let's eat before we upset Mrs Murrel." Lana stood and went to load her plate up with Rory close behind.

Bram looked at Aoife trying to gauge her mood. "You, okay?"

"I am actually. Your family are lovely, and I think I want to take Mrs Murrel home."

"Good luck. Lana will fight you for her."

When Titan and Snow arrived, talk turned to the estate and what there was to do. Titan decided he'd go with Rory and check out the cattle while Snow would stay back and look around the castle. As a former jewel and fine art thief, Snow had a huge appreciation for antiques and artwork, and they had a lot here in the castle. Some would say he was a fool for trusting her with such temptation, but he did. Snow had never stolen to be bad, she'd done it because it was all she knew to survive until Jack had found her and given her the same choices he had the rest. Finding her people, as she called Shadow, had been enough to break the habit.

Having Snow with Lana and Titan with Rory also achieved two other goals, and that was to make sure they were each safe and had someone with them and gave him some time alone with Aoife.

"You ready to have a look around?"

"Yes. Is this okay?" She motioned at her clothing, jeans and a jumper with a gilet over top.

"Yeah, we can grab you some wellies on the way out."

Ushering her toward the door he saw a smiling Mrs M watching them from the hallway as she dusted the table. A nod and a wink of approval made him smile. He didn't know what he and Aoife had yet, but he knew he was glad to have the seal of approval from those he loved.

He wished his parents could have met her and wondered what they would've made of all this. The letter from his father still sat in his bag where he'd stuffed it last minute before leaving to head home with Aoife.

"Ready to go?"

Bram's head snapped up and he saw the pink of excitement in Aoife's cheeks. It was a look he hadn't seen before, but it suited her, and he knew he wanted to see more of it. "Sure, let's go."

CHAPTER 18

"Oh my God, I can't believe that cow chased us."

Bram still had hold of her hand, where he'd grabbed it when the beast had run at them. "She was just curious, and then you screamed and scared her."

"I scared her?" Aoife was pointing her finger at her chest. "I almost died, and I got mud inside my boot."

Bram pulled her against him and wrapped his arm around her, kissing her head. This morning had been damn near perfect. Showing the estate to someone who had no idea about the history and seeing it for the first time through their eyes had awoken his love for his home.

"You were not even close to dying, you daft mare."

"Daft mare am I? Well, I'll show you."

He saw the playful glint in her eye seconds before she shoved him, and he went flying backwards into a mud puddle, landing on his ass. Shock rendered him speechless but when he looked up to see Aoife bent double with laughter, he knew he'd happily let her do it again if it kept that smile on her face.

"Oh, you're in so much trouble now."

Aoife's eyes widened and she took off running through the woods as he gave chase. She darted through the trees, making so much noise even a blind and deaf person could find her. The density of the redwoods and the oaks in this part of the forest made the atmosphere seem darker than it was.

He saw Aoife dart behind a fallen oak, ducking down so she wouldn't be found. Doubling back, he went around the long way, keeping her in his sights as she tried and failed to hide from him. Sneaking up from behind, he deliberately stepped on a branch not wanting to scare her given all she'd been through.

Aoife shrieked with laughter as she spun on her heel and saw him, taking off running. He grabbed her, taking them to the ground, rolling so she landed on him and not the cold, damp forest floor.

"Got ya."

He held tight as she wriggled, and his fingers tickled her sides, making her giggle.

"No, stop. Oh God. I hate being tickled."

"But you're laughing." He kept going making her squirm and giggle.

"I know, it's a reaction."

Bram stopped but regretted it when she sat up with a giggled sigh, her knees on either side of his hips. Feeling her warm heat against his dick was heaven and hell at the same time. His hands skimmed her muscled thighs, her hands landed on his chest. God, he wanted to kiss her, to taste her again, to feel her body as it squeezed his cock as she came apart.

Aoife rocked against his hard dick, and he cursed, the feeling so good and knowing how spectacular it was between them.

"Aoife, I'm only human. So if you don't want me to pin you to this cold ground and make you scream with my tongue on that tight pussy, then I suggest you move."

He saw the desire darken her eyes and then the reality of where they were seemed to come to her, and she stood slowly. Bram took her hand as she reached to pull him up and used it to pull her against his chest. "Slow, remember," he murmured against her lips.

"I know, but it feels so natural with you."

"I know it does, baby, so let it go at its own pace. No rush, no expectations. Let's just do what feels right."

"Can I kiss you?"

Bram cocooned her in his arms, his palms resting on her lower back as he smirked down at her. "You can kiss me any damn time you please."

"Good."

Then he felt her lips brush against his, tentative at first, nothing like the woman he'd met at the pub, who had seemed so sure of what she wanted. This Aoife was cautious as if she was learning what she liked and who she was for the first time instead of playing a role assigned to her. He was happy to let her experiment, to find out who she was because he knew who she was inside, and this morning had only solidified how he felt for her.

He let her take the lead at first, her head slanting as she deepened the connection, her tongue moving against his as she became more confident. When her hands gripped his back he took over, guiding her, taking the kiss deeper. His teeth nipped at her bottom lip, making her gasp and push closer to his body until they were both moaning and desperate for more. Wanting to honour her wishes, he pulled away and buried his head in her neck, nipping the skin with his teeth making her yelp.

"Minx, you're trying to kill me."

"Never, but I do think we should get out of these clothes." Bram's face lit up and she laughed. "Not like that, but because we stink of god knows what."

Bram looked down at his clothes and grimaced. "Good idea. Then we can go into the village and get some lunch."

Aoife wrinkled her nose and knocked her head against his

shoulder as they walked back to the castle hand in hand. "Sounds good."

Stumbling in through the boot room, they were met by Lana and Snow who were just coming in through the library door.

Lana rushed to him, excitement on her face. "Oh my god, Bram. You won't believe this, but you know that picture in the library above the fire?"

"The one that looks like the kids did it at nursery?"

Lana shook her head then nodded. "Yes, that one. Well, you won't believe this, but Snow says it an original Jackson Pollock and worth millions."

Bram glanced at Snow who confirmed it. "No way. That piece of crap? I could paint better than that."

"Neanderthal, you wouldn't know art if it bit you on the ass."

He could tell Snow wasn't impressed as she took her art very seriously. "Maybe, but I know what I like."

"Yeah, yeah, whatever."

"Well, if you're happy then that's great but you might want to let the insurance people know and have it verified by an appraiser."

"Oh, god you're right. I need to get on that now."

Lana rushed down the hallway as fast as her pregnant belly allowed, and he wondered if she slowed down even long enough to give birth or if she was issuing orders from her bed as she pushed.

"Not to be a bitch or anything but you two stink!" Snow was backing away from them, and it only made Aoife laugh, making him laugh too. "Okay, I have no idea what is going on here but you two have obviously found some crazy mushrooms out in the wilderness. I'll be in the library when you're ready to go into town."

"We'll be about half an hour. Is Titan back yet?"

"Yeah, he went back to the house to change as he slipped in some mud."

Bram shook his head. "You townies."

Snow lifted her middle finger as she walked away, making him chuckle.

"Race you upstairs. Last one up buys lunch."

Bram saw the competitive nature switch on in Aoife and gave her a split second head start before chasing after her. This was fun and easy, but he needed to make sure he didn't lose sight of why they were there and the goal, which was to end Jimmy Doyle. Maybe then Aoife could be free and they could figure out if they had a future.

CHAPTER 19

THE VILLAGE OF MCCULLUM WAS PICTURE-POSTCARD BEAUTIFUL, EVEN MORE so up close. Aoife could see from one side of the main street to the other it was so small, but every building seemed to have its own personality. "What was it like growing up here?"

Bram was holding her hand as they walked, Snow and Titan just a few steps behind them as they chatted. "Honestly, I hated it."

Aoife raised her brows at his answer.

"I was fine when I was a kid, but as I reached my teens, I failed to see the beauty and only saw the lack of anything to do. There was no cinema, big shops, or arcades. Every person here knew me, so I couldn't do anything without it getting back to my parents."

"I get that, but you seem to love it now."

"I do. It took being away for me to appreciate what I have here. I'd always loved the outdoors and I lived for rock climbing, shooting, camping, anything to do with the wilderness so I ended up spending lots of time doing that. My friends and I would camp in the forest and take girls down to the lake."

"Oh, a bad boy, were you?"

Bram grimaced. "Let's put it this way. If I ever have a daughter, she's not dating a boy like me."

Aoife laughed. "You want kids, Bram?"

"I don't know. Sometimes I feel I do then I think of the life I lead and know it wouldn't be fair for a family to be forced into that life."

"You won't do this forever though, surely?"

"No, I guess not. What about you?"

"Yes, I want kids. I always vowed I'd give them the freedom and choices I never had."

"You'll be a great mum."

Aoife glanced at him as they stopped outside a bakery. "You think?"

"Yeah. You're strong, loving, kind. What more could you want?"

"I hope I'm strong enough."

Bram cupped her face. "Are you kidding? You're the fucking strongest person I know." He kissed her then, slow and drugging and she sank into it, wanting more. Catcalling from behind broke them apart and Aoife blushed at Snow who was pretending to gag.

"Get a room, you two."

"Abraham McCullum, is that you making out on my doorstep?"

Aoife and Bram turned to see an older woman wearing a green and white blouse, a green cardigan, and a plaid skirt, with her white hair pulled back into a bun at the base of her neck.

"Mrs Clark, it's so good to see you." Bram let go of her hand to hug the woman who seemed pleased to see him.

"Aye, laddie, it's good to see you too. Been way too long ye been gone from us."

"Well, it's only a flying visit, but I wanted my friends to taste some of your delicious pineapple tarts."

"Well, why didn't ye say so?" Mrs Clark pulled Bram in through the door by the sleeve and motioned for them to take a seat. "Now, will you be having tea?"

Bram looked at her and she nodded. "Yes, please."

Mrs Clark looked at Snow and Titan. "And what can I get you both?"

Titan was already looking over the small menu. "What would you recommend?"

"Well, a big lad like you needs his fuel, so I think a meat pie and then some of my famous Dundee cake."

"Sounds great, and may I have a coffee to go with that please?"

"Och, with manners like that, you can have whatever you wish."

Mrs Clark took the rest of the orders, smiling wide when Snow ordered the same as Titan.

"I like a girl who can eat. Are you married, lass? My Johnny is still single."

Snow blushed and said she was in fact single.

"Snow here is headed home in a few days. Unfortunately, Mrs Clark, the matchmaking is a bust this time." Bram gently helped a panicked looking Snow from her corner.

"Well, I tell ye if he keeps on messing around, he's never gonna find a nice lass like you seemed to have."

Bram hugged Aoife closer and she snuggled into him as he kissed her head. "I'm a lucky man."

"'Tis good to have you back, Bram. We've missed you around these parts."

"It's good to be home, Mrs Clark."

With a smile, she rushed off to get the food sorted and Aoife looked at Bram, really seeing how much he fit into this place and how much everyone who knew him loved him, told a lot about the man he was.

"Abraham?" Snow's eyes sparkled with mischief.

"Don't you start."

Her smirk told him that she was saving that for another day.

"So, are there any women's clothing shops around here?" Snow looked down at her boots, which had seen better days. "I figure I need some new boots and a new coat."

"Yes, two doors down is Mrs Price. She should have everything you need."

"Want to go after we finish eating, Aoife?"

"Yes, sure. I need a few items too."

The pineapple tart had been amazing and nothing like she'd ever tasted before. Titan had been equally effusive about the meat pies. Once she and Snow had finished, they left Bram and Titan, who headed for the general store, and made their way to the clothing shop.

As soon as they walked in it was clear the woman knew who she was, and they were greeted like long lost friends.

"If you need anything, just give me a shout."

"Thank you."

Snow giggled. "This is nuts. I can't believe we didn't know Bram was practically royal. They treat him like he's a returning hero."

"I know, they do love him."

"I heard one of the people at the castle saying how much his family gives to the village and if it wasn't for the Castle, they wouldn't make a living, and because of Lana and the changes she and Rory have made, that their own children are returning to raise their families here."

"Really? You learned that after a day, Snow?"

Snow shrugged. "What? I hear things."

"Um, so what about you? Bram was a closet Laird. What are you hiding?" Aoife tried on a blue coat, which was thick and warm, but Snow shook her head giving it the heave-ho.

"What's to say? Not royal or titled, no Cinderella story here. I was a thief growing up. My family was a waste of space and then Jack saved me."

"Jack saved you?"

Snow handed her a deep burgundy coat to try on as she tried an ice-blue one. "Yeah, but don't ask me anymore because I can't answer, and I like you."

Aoife rolled her eyes. "So, you don't want to have to kill me?"

Snow laughed. "What the hell is wrong with you? No, because I can't tell you without permission and I hate confrontation."

"Oh." Aoife liked the red coat and chose some brown knee-high riding-style boots to go with it.

"Seriously who do you think we are?"

"Um, trained mercenaries, killers, super spies, all of the above."

Snow tipped her head. "See that's why I like you. You said all that with a straight face and it didn't faze you in the slightest."

"I figured you wouldn't be helping me only to hurt me, so I'm taking it all at face value." Aoife popped her stuff on the counter as Mrs Price came from the back. "Plus, I like you too. All of you, even Lotus, although the verdict is still out on Bás."

"Bás is complex, but he's loyal."

"Shall I bag these up for you ladies?"

"Yes, please." Aoife went to hand over some cash, the last of her savings and Mrs Price shook her head.

"No need, lassie. Mr Bram had taken care of it for you both."

"Get in." Snow said with a smile.

Aoife shook her head. "Thank you."

They left the shop and saw Bram waiting outside the butchers with Titan, who had a bag in his hand.

They crossed the road, if it could even be called that, and she walked straight into Bram's arms and kissed him.

His arms came around her and he held her close. "What was that for?"

"For being amazing and buying me these things, and so much more I can't ever thank you for."

"Don't make me hose you two down for public indecency," Snow warned with a stern look, just as the first splash of rain hit Aoife on the nose.

"We should head back before the heavens open and we get soaked."

They ran for the car and Bram drove them back to the castle, dropping Titan and Snow back at the house they were using. The rain was coming down in sheets now as the afternoon darkened.

"Wanna get a hot chocolate in front of the fire and then I have a surprise for you?"

"You do? What is it?" Aoife could hardly keep still in her seat at the thought of a surprise for her.

Bram grinned, making her tummy flutter wildly. God, he was so beautiful, he could have been a model and that was with clothes on. Without them, he was a freaking god.

"If I tell you, it won't be a surprise, but it's a cool one, I promise."

Aoife clapped her hands like a little kid. "Yes, I want a surprise."

He stopped the car in front of the castle but at the back this time, instead of the impressive front entrance.

Holding his jacket over their heads, they ran for the back door, falling inside laughing like two kids and she wondered if she'd ever been happier. On the back of that thought came the worry that it would all end and she'd be back in her empty hell. Pushing it away, she vowed to hold on to this time and this man with everything she had.

CHAPTER 20

Bram watched Aoife as she sipped her hot chocolate made by Mrs Murrel. He'd tried to make it but found himself pushed out of the kitchen. Probably for the best. Mrs M was so much better than he was at it, and she'd added a dram of whisky to warm them both up.

Aoife moaned at the first sip, and he found himself having to discreetly adjust his jeans. Spending today with her had been perfect. She'd been open and free, relaxed and smiling, and he found himself imagining what it would be like if this was their life more and more.

Would he be satisfied living here full time if it meant being with the woman he'd admitted to himself he was falling in love with? Seeing the simple joy she took in the smallest things made his chest tighten and warm. Watching her with the villagers, who he'd grown up knowing and seeing how they took to her, made him realise that he wasn't the only one who saw it either.

Titan had admitted he'd been unsure at first if he was making a mistake getting involved, and he'd almost voted against helping her but in the end, he'd trusted that Bram saw something worth saving, and now he saw it too. Titan was a good man deep down despite the bad things he'd done in his previous life. He also saw how protective Titan was of Snow. They partnered together a lot, seeming to work well as a team. He wondered if there was more to it than just friends and hoped that wasn't the case, team members getting involved was strictly forbidden and he would hate to lose either of them.

Aoife had changed again into an oversized jumper and leggings with thick socks on her feet. She looked cosy and relaxed and so fucking sexy he could hardly keep from reaching for her, but he'd promised her they'd go at a natural pace. He just felt his pace was increasing and wasn't sure if hers was.

"You ready for your surprise?"

"Oh, thank God. I was trying to be cool, but I'm so excited."

Bram rubbed his scruff. "Now I feel I may have oversold this. It's not that exciting."

"Just show me already."

Bram pulled her up and helped her slip her boots back on. "I bet you were a nightmare on Christmas Eve, weren't you?"

"Oh, totally. My mum had to lie with me until I fell asleep right up until I was eleven. I just couldn't contain my excitement and then I couldn't sleep."

"You were close?"

"Yeah, we were. She died of cancer when I was a teenager. I miss her every day, but it's her voice in my head that keeps me going."

"I'm glad you had that."

"Me too."

Bram walked with her hand in hand down the hallway and past the kitchen and up the stairs toward the rooms on the east side where they were staying.

Aoife chuckled. "Is this surprise in my bedroom?"

"It is, but it isn't what you might be thinking."

"It isn't?"

Bram huffed out a laugh as he tried not to let his mind go in that direction. "No, although now I kind of wish it was."

Pushing open her door, he stepped inside and closed it before walking to the window. Pushing aside the heavy brocade, he pressed his hand against the wall and felt the click. Aoife was watching him wide-eyed, and he loved that she was shocked in a good way for a change.

Pushing the secret door open, he revealed a small space behind the exterior wall. Using the light on his phone to light the way, he took her hand and drew her in before closing the door behind them.

"A secret passage. Are you freaking kidding? This is the coolest thing ever."

"I thought you might like it."

It was barely wide enough for him to fit through and he had to duck his head a lot. Cobwebs hung off the stone walls as they descended, the decline sharper as he knew they were headed for the ground floor.

"Where does this lead?"

"You'll see."

They came to a fork, and he pointed his light to the left. "That leads to my father's office. There's a door behind his bookshelf."

Her hand squeezed his and he glanced back to see her smiling from ear to ear. "What were these used for?"

"When the castle was built, Scotland was at war with England. They built the tunnels so the noble families wouldn't get trapped if there was an attack."

"Wow, this is so cool."

He stopped to point his phone at the wall as they rounded a sharp bend. "See this?" He pointed out the markings he knew by heart, his finger running over them, almost feeling the history in the walls. "This is the crest of King James II of Scotland. He was led through these tunnels to safety when his father King James I was assassinated. His mother, Queen Joan, then got to him and he was crowned King at the age of six."

He watched Aoife touch the markings with reverence and knew she understood the magnitude of the history here. "If these walls could talk."

"I know. I have hundreds of stories passed down from my father, not all of them show our ancestors in the best light but they're our history."

"I don't think there's a person on the planet who can say they're proud of every action their kin have taken if you go back far enough."

"No, I think that's right."

"Why didn't you want to rule the Estate or whatever the right term is?" They continued walking as he led her through and around the maze of tunnels, pointing out different markings.

"Honestly, for a long time I never felt worthy and then it was overwhelming. If you could see the way the people loved my father you'd understand. I didn't want the responsibility of it all and it had been heaped on my shoulders from such a young age. I would've done it. I was going to take my place and do what was expected, and then my life took a turn I wasn't expecting, and it all went to hell."

Bram hated talking about this, hated remembering his failure. How he'd let his family down. His throat clogged as he tried to find the words to explain it all, to tell the woman he cared about how he was no better than a common criminal, how he'd killed a man in cold blood with his rage, and worse, he'd do it again.

"It's okay, you don't have to tell me."

He pulled her to the exit of the tunnels, his movements more urgent now as he felt the walls close in around him, his breaths coming faster. Pushing out into the cold, fresh air of the night, he sucked in a lungful of oxygen, letting the outdoors calm him in a way nothing else could.

"It's not that I don't want to, I do. I just can't right now."

Aoife laid a hand on his back and her touch grounded him. "I understand, Bram. God knows there are things I can't talk about, and you'll get no judgement from me. So, if and when you're ready, I'll listen, but if not that's okay too."

Looking down at her in wonder, he wondered what good he'd done in life for the universe to send him such an amazing person. His fingertips skimmed her lips, and he heard the sharp intake of her breath. "Where did you come from?"

"Same place as you, I guess."

"I feel like every second with you is a blessing I don't deserve and yet I wouldn't swap a single minute of it for a lifetime with someone else."

Tears welled in her eyes. "Bram."

"Sorry, didn't mean to make you cry. Was it that cheesy?"

"So cheesy, like double mozzarella and cheddar, but also the most beautiful thing anyone has ever said to me."

"Can I ask, though, why put me in the room with a tunnel? Weren't you afraid I might find it?"

"Because I never want you to feel trapped again, Aoife. I want you to know you always have a way to get out, to run if you feel if you have to."

Her hiccupped sob stole his breath as she leaned into him. Bram kissed her, slow heat building between them in the cool of the night.

"I want you, Bram."

"Thank fuck."

He led her up the stairs quickly, bypassing his own room in favour of hers, knowing she felt comfortable there.

Locking the door with the key, he led her to the fire, leaving her to sit in the chair while he stoked the flames. Standing, he moved toward where she sat on the chaise and gazed down at her. Cupping her cheek, his thumb rubbed over her bottom lip before pushing into her mouth. Closing her eyes, she sucked his thumb deep, making him wish it was his cock and a hiss escaped him at the vision in front of him, so seductive and perfect.

Her eyes opened, heavy-lidded desire, the jade almost emerald in the firelight. He could watch her all night and never get sick of the sight or feel of her.

"I can't stop thinking about you, of this."

His admission seemed to be like a match igniting the flame of desire that had been burning low in both of them all day. Fuck, since he'd left her bed over ten days ago. Aoife moved her hands to his belt, making quick work of the buckle, the loud clink of metal the only sound apart from their breathing. Bram held his breath, not wanting to break the erotic spell she was weaving on him.

With her eyes still on his, she undid his belt, her tongue twirling around his thumb imitating what she'd do to his cock. Bram held still, the desire to take over strong, but the need to see her take control even stronger.

Her hand found his cock, hard and straining as she slipped it inside his jeans and cupped his length before releasing him from the confines of his jeans and boxers. She stroked his cock, from root to tip, slowly, making his hips buck as pleasure slithered down his spine, making his balls ache. Bram was done being a bystander, removing his thumb from her hot mouth to the neck of her jumper, he pushed it down, exposing her navy lace bra. Fuck she was hot, her skin flushed with arousal from his touch.

An ache started inside him, and he roughly pushed the lace aside and gripped her nipple with his forefinger and thumb. He twisted her nipple hard causing her to throw her head back on a moan. His girl was a naughty one, she liked it rough and liked it when he made demands on her, and he remembered the way she'd got so wet when he talked dirty, telling her what he wanted from her.

"Suck me, Irish."

His gravelly words, demanding and dark made her moan as she wrapped her lips around the head of his cock. A hiss fell from his lips at the first touch of her warm, wet mouth on his crown.

Aoife looked up to him, her eyes dark with pleasure to see him watching her as she worked him over.

Heaven, he was in fucking heaven as she worked him over, alternating between soft gentle torturous licks to taking him so deep he hit the back of her throat. His hands continued playing with her perfect tits, making her squirm as he rolled the tight buds between his fingers.

His free hand gripped her hair tight, and he knew she loved the burn on her scalp because she moaned around his cock, almost making him lose his damn mind with pleasure. Bram thrust forward, his cock driving down her throat until her lips touched his pelvis, holding there for a second before he moved back, allowing her to catch her breath. Something about the raw desire she evoked in him made him feel powerless and that was something he hadn't felt in a long time. Yet he didn't care, because here in this room, he was happy to let her have control if this was the result.

As her movements became quicker, she cupped his balls, rolling them in her hand as he growled her name in warning, his come bubbling in his balls as his orgasm raced towards the finish line. Aoife ignored it, redoubling her efforts as he lost control, his seed exploding from him on a roar, his knees almost buckling with the pleasure of it.

Bram staggered back as he pulled out, and she wiped her mouth with the back of her hand. Even that was hot, seeing her looking so dishevelled from sucking his cock.

Bram tucked his softening cock back into his jeans and pulled her to stand before him.

"That was fucking sensational, Aoife." His lips found hers and he kissed her slowly. "But I'm not done with you yet. I'm going to make you come so hard you won't remember your own name, and then I'm going to fuck you in front of the fire until neither of us can stand."

"I can't wait to have you inside me again. I've missed you."

"I've missed you too, Irish."

Aoife stroked his cheek, rubbing the rough stubble on his face against her fingertips.

Bram lifted her into his arms and carried her toward the bed, laying her down softly before falling to his knees on the floor. Pulling the boots from her feet, he tossed them behind him. Next, he peeled her leggings from her body, admiring the lace underwear she wore as his fingers skimmed her skin.

"So soft. Your skin is the softest thing I've ever felt."

Aoife didn't reply because he was kissing his way up her thighs, over her hips, avoiding the place he knew she wanted him most and a smirk played on his lips at her groan of displeasure. He drew her jumper over her head, threading his arm behind her to release the catch on her bra. Her breasts spilled free and his dick twitched in interest.

He worshipped her body, kissing every part of her exposed skin, his teeth biting at her nipples in a way he knew she liked. As she writhed, he could feel his dick hardening as it pushed from his open jeans.

Finally, he'd tortured her enough and his lips landed on the crease of her thigh, right beside her pussy. Pushing the lace to the side, he swiped his tongue through her folds, and she arched off the bed at the contact. When he swiped his tongue over her clit, a keening moan erupted from her, as her fingers clenched the sheets and her climax washed over her as she pulsed against his lips.

Gently he pushed two fingers inside her tight pussy finding her soaking wet as her walls tried to clamp down on his fingers.

Wasting no more time, he stood, smiling at her outraged expression, and shed his clothes. His dick jumped in excitement as she watched him roll a condom down his length.

Putting a knee in the bed, he made space between her hips and her leg curled around his back trying to get him closer. A knot of desire grew as he bent, his mouth seizing hers in a deep, hungry kiss as the slow lovemaking became a dark need that chased them both, leaving a tangled mess of desperate need in him. He thrust inside her, not stopping until he was buried to the hilt, and she cried out, her hands clawing at his back.

Bram groaned, the pleasure-pain of her passion consuming him as he fucked her hard and raw. Threading his fingers through hers, he held her hands above her head, lifting her tits to his mouth and as he fucked her, he sucked her nipple into his mouth, causing her to rock back against him, their bodies in sync as they chased the same thing.

"Bram."

"What, baby? What do you need?"

"More, harder."

"Fuck me, you're perfect."

Bram had never fucked gentle, and he loved the raw animalistic fucking between them, but he almost loved the gentle side as much. She was perfect in every way. She was his and he'd burn down the world before he let anyone take her from him.

As his climax built, he twisted his hips, hitting her clit with his pelvic bone and her walls tightened around his dick, almost strangling him until he saw stars and her cry of pleasure set off his own orgasm.

As his movements slowed, he captured her lips in a long, slow kiss. Pulling away he saw her smiling her eyes closed. "You good?"

"Yep." Her voice was mellow, her face relaxed as he pulled away.

"Be right back."

He dealt with the condom and walked back to the bedroom, climbing in beside Aoife and pulling her into his arms as she draped over him like a human blanket.

"I think I died and went to heaven."

Bram barked a laugh as he squeezed her butt cheek.

Aoife snuggled closer, her leg flopping over his waist. "When can we do that again?"

Bram looked down at her in awe as she tried to hide her face in his chest. "Get some rest, Irish, while I regain my strength. Then I'll wake you with my mouth between your legs."

"Sounds like a plan."

Bram held her in his arms as she let sleep take her, knowing that in the space of twenty-four hours he'd gone from not knowing if he could make it work between them, to knowing he couldn't live without this woman. He wondered if it was how Rory felt about Lana and Jack about Astrid. He didn't know but knew he'd end the life of anyone who ever tried to hurt her again, and if that made him a monster then so be it.

CHAPTER 21

After three weeks of silence with no threats from her father or signs of his men, Aoife was beginning to relax. Spending most of her days helping either Lana or Mrs Murrel, she was growing to love it there. She'd figured she had a talent for baking and loved learning new recipes and Mrs Murrel loved to show her, passing on little tips that she wished she'd been able to learn from her own mother.

Snow and Titan were still there and spent a lot of time around the estate, some with Bram, other times doing their own thing. She'd liked getting to know Lana and Snow, not having had many friends her own age apart from Peyton, who she'd only spoken to once since they left Longtown.

Her nights were spent with Bram. He was insatiable, which was perfect because she couldn't get enough of him. He was tender, sweet, but also had a dark edge which she loved. She was never sure if he was going to make love to her or fuck her and she loved both. Sex had gone from being something she could take or leave to something she craved, although she was sure it was the man himself who she craved.

"You ready to go?"

Aoife looked up to see Bram waiting in the kitchen door, a bag slung over his back.

"We're going somewhere?"

He moved closer, wrapping his hand around the ponytail she wore and tilting her head back, his teeth nipping her bottom lip. "I want to show you something."

Aoife smirked. "Oh, yeah, I think I've heard that line before, and I've seen it." Her hand snaked between them and cupped his dick, which hardened beneath her hand.

The hiss from his lips vibrated along her jaw as he rocked his body against her. "Much as I want to take you upstairs and make use of this hard-on you created, I want to show you this more."

Intrigued now, Aoife pulled away.

"Get a warm coat and boots on. We're going outside."

Aoife did both and Bram met her at the door with a quad bike.

"I'm not getting on that death trap!"

Bram chuckled. "Don't be dramatic."

Aoife climbed on behind him and held on for dear life. "If I die, I'm coming back to haunt you."

Bram turned his head to look at her. "I won't let you die, Irish." The look he gave her was determined and Aoife wondered if he was still talking about the quad bike or something else.

Bram drove them skilfully over the hilly terrain of the estate, heading deeper into the woods than they'd gone before. The day was cold, with frost hanging onto the trees, the sun bright but freezing, making it seem beautiful, like a Christmas card.

Stopping the bike, he helped her off the back and retrieved the rucksack from the compartment under the seat.

"We need to walk from here."

Grabbing her hand, they set off through the woods, with Bram pointing out different tracks in the mud. Showing her which berries she could eat safely and even finding some mushrooms which were safe to eat, that he bagged up to take back for Mrs Murrel.

"You love it here, don't you?"

Bram looked ahead of him over the expanse of land that fell off into a valley on the left, the trees thinning now as they left the safety of the woods. "I do and I don't. I love the nature, the history, the freedom, but I hate the expectation. I wasn't built to be a Laird of the manor. I do what I do with Shadow because I'm good at it and because I love it." He glanced at her and seemed to be steeling himself to say something. "I don't want you getting the wrong idea about me, Aoife. I'm not a good man, not in the true sense."

Aoife stilled as he kept walking for a few steps, before turning back to her. "What does that even mean?"

"It means I've killed people and will again."

Aoife took a step back as Bram stepped forward, his hand outstretched. "Not you, Aoife. I'd never harm a hair on your head, but the job I do, the people we go after are evil, and the world is a better place without them in it. I have no trouble ending them to keep good people safe and untouched by the horrors of the world."

Aoife felt herself relax at his words. "I understand that, Bram. I won't pretend to know what you do, but I get why you do it. So many people believe that life is black and white, but it isn't. It's radiant colour and shades of grey. There'll always be a need for pure people who uphold the law, but without men and women like you and the others from Shadow, they couldn't do that. You keep the monsters at bay so we can all sleep easy."

She walked toward him, laying her hands on his chest as he embraced her. "How did I get so lucky as to find you?"

"I think I found you, mister."

"Whatever, but thank you for getting me, for understanding me."

"You may not see yourself as good, Bram, but I've seen people pretend to be good who have the blackest souls and you don't pretend. Your heart is pure, and I know every life you take is for a reason. In my book that makes you purer than any fake do-gooder."

Bram kissed her and it was slow and deep, and she knew she was falling in love with this complex man who thought he was bad but hid a heart of pure gold.

He took her hand and they continued walking, Bram occasionally looking to the skyline where clouds had begun to gather. "We won't be able to stay as long as I'd hoped. A storm is rolling in."

"That's okay, it's just nice to get out and enjoy the air."

They walked for a bit more, the land opening up in front of them as the trees thinned. The rushing sound of water told her they were close to a river. They rounded a corner and Aoife's breath escaped her. A large reservoir or lake was backed up against the mountain-side and the rushing of a waterfall, tipping over the side into the lake, was exposed.

It was stunning and she wished had a camera so she could capture the vista before her. "Oh wow, it's magnificent." Bram, who must have seen it a hundred times growing up, seemed equally inspired by the sight before them. "This place is a gift. You have no idea how lucky you are to have this on your doorstep."

"I do, which is why I know it's safer with Lana and Rory. I break things, Irish. I drop the ball on everything and I couldn't let it happen with this place."

Aoife hated that he didn't see himself for the man she knew he was, but she also realised that it wasn't something he'd hear if she told him. He'd need to learn that by himself, she just wished she knew how to help him see it.

They spent the morning and into the early afternoon by the water, eating the still warm breakfast rolls Bram had made and drinking hot chocolate to keep the chill out.

As they walked back to the quad bike, the rain began to fall, the sky darkening, but none of that could take away the enjoyment of the morning they'd spent together.

"Thank you for showing me this place."

Bram twined his fingers with hers. "We should come back in the summer when we can swim without getting frostbite."

Inside Aoife was screaming with excitement that he thought they'd still be together in the summer. Lost in thought she didn't see the tree stump and tripped, turning her ankle as Bram saved her from actually falling. Crying out in pain, she went to put weight on her left foot and winced as agony shot through her ankle and knee, all the way to her hip.

"Jesus, Aoife, are you okay?"

"I think I sprained my ankle or knee they both hurt like hell."

"Here, sit down let me take a look."

Bram helped her sit on a fallen tree stump and rolled her trouser leg up so he could see it. She didn't need a doctor to tell her she'd sprained her ankle and her knee had some swelling too; she'd had enough broken bones in her time to know it wasn't broken. The rain was coming down heavy now, soaking them through the gaps in the trees and making her shiver.

"It's just a sprain." Bram looked at her with a thunderous expression, so she relented. "Fine, have a look."

Bram began gently feeling her leg, making her wince as he slipped off her boot, the limb already swelling. Great, she wasn't getting that boot back on now.

"It might be a sprain but I think you may have fractured your metatarsal and twisted your knee."

"Great, just what I need."

"We need to get back before we get soaked through and the least of our worries will be your leg. Can you walk if I help you?"

Aoife gritted her teeth with the pain and nodded as Bram helped her to stand, taking most of her weight. They hobbled at a ridiculously slow pace and she knew she needed to pick it up or they'd be stuck in this freezing cold all night and most likely die of exposure.

"I'm sorry."

"What for?"

"Ruining our lovely day."

"Don't be silly, it was an accident. Unless your plan all along was to get me alone in the woods so you could have your way with me?"

Aoife laughed through the discomfort. "Shit, you've seen through my nefarious plan."

"Nefarious, hey?"

"Oh yes, complete evil genius mastermind here."

Bram raised an eyebrow at her, and she was glad he was distracting her from the cold and the pain.

They finally reached the quad and Aoife thought she'd never been so relieved to see a death trap.

"Here, hold on tight and I'll get us back to the castle and then we can get your leg x-rayed."

She would've argued but she didn't want to waste precious time when she could be in the warm. With fingers she could hardly feel from cold, Aoife held on to Bram, her teeth chattering as he drove them through the now dark woods toward the castle.

CHAPTER 22

"I CAN WALK YOU KNOW."

Bram ignored Aoife's protest and swung her up into his arms. "I know, but this is quicker."

He settled her into the back of the vehicle, at least now she had dry clothes on and had warmed up from the drenching they'd both got. He shouldn't have taken her out there, but he'd been eager for her to see his favourite spot on the estate. The last three weeks being there with her had changed things for him. He'd never been in love before, but he was certainly headed down that road with Irish.

Warning her about the man he really was underneath the one she saw was as much for him as her. She made him forget the bad he'd done, the lives he'd taken and would take. He knew he wasn't a psychopath, but it took a certain type of person to be in Shadow and he was happy with who he was. He just needed her to understand who that was before she got more involved.

He pulled up outside the hospital in Inverness, Snow and Titan in the car behind, making sure they didn't pick up a tail and watching his back while they got Aoife's injury looked at. He knew they were armed with the latest in weaponry and he could see just by the shift in their demeanour that they were alert for any threats.

Bein walked to the desk and smiled down at the young receptionist. "Hi, my girlfriend hurt her ankle and knee."

The blonde smiled back a flirty look on her face as she completely ignored Aoife, which irritated him no end, and if the steam coming from Irish's ears was any suggestion, then she was pissed too. It made him want to smile but as he didn't have a death wish he remained perfectly proper.

"Oh, poor thing. Name?"

"Debbie Smith."

He'd already had Watchdog build in a fake identity that would be perfect for this situation.

"Address?"

Bein rattled off the address they'd decided on, answering the rest of the questions quickly.

"And how did it happen?"

"She slipped on a tree root."

"You really should be more careful when you get older."

Bein grabbed Aoife around the waist as she went to move forward, probably to give the woman a piece of her mind.

He brought his lips to her ear. "Cool it, slugger. We don't want her to remember us and you punching her lights out might hinder that."

Aoife angled her face to him, her eyes bright with fire and he wanted nothing more than to kiss her until neither of them could breathe. "Then maybe you should quit flirting with her."

Bein smirked and kissed her cheek. He fucking loved her fiery side as much as the sweet one and how it had come out more in the last few weeks, showing him who she really was.

Turning back to the receptionist he cleared the smile from his face and gave her a hard look. "How long will it be?"

"It depends on what comes in, but the wait is around an hour at the moment."

"Thank you."

He walked Aoife over to a hard plastic chair in the corner away from others with Snow and Titan positioned so that nobody could get close to them. He was fairly confident Doyle hadn't found them, but he wasn't taking any chances.

He dropped a kiss on her head as he wrapped a protective arm around Aoife.

"You doing okay?"

"Yeah, just hate making a fuss. I'm sure it's fine."

"Maybe but I want to make sure and you're not making the fuss, I am."

Aoife cocked an eyebrow at him. "That's true. You're a bit of an old woman sometimes with your fussing."

The smirk on her face told him the ibuprofen he'd given her was working and the pain had let up. It also let him know he was forgiven for his non-flirting with the receptionist. Aoife wasn't afraid of him and was happy to tease him or call him out on things and he liked that about her. He didn't want a wallflower; he wanted an equal, and until now he'd never even realised that.

"An old woman! I'll show you old woman later when I get you home."

"Promises, promises."

Bein laughed; his head thrown back with humour. This woman was going to be the death of him, and he wouldn't have it any other way.

It took an hour but eventually, they were called back and a young doctor looked at Aoife's leg, prodding and pressing before he decided he needed an X-ray on her ankle and knee. That involved more waiting around followed by sitting in the cubicle waiting for the doctor to read the scan. The curtain pulled back and Bein tensed, his hand going for his sidearm before he relaxed seeing the doctor with his head buried in the papers he was holding.

"It seems you've fractured one of the small bones in your foot and twisted your knee. We can give you crutches to help you walk and you need to wear sensible, flat shoes or boots for a while. Keep the leg elevated and rest it for a few days."

Bein hated the thought of her in any pain. "What about pain relief?"

"I can give her something but over the counter pain medication should suffice. I did want to ask you about the implant in your leg though, Ms Smith."

Bein felt his entire body go cold, every cell and synapsis waking up and sensing danger. Aoife looked at him blankly and he knew in that second exactly how Doyle had been tracking her.

"Implant?"

"Yes, in your right thigh, just above your knee. The technicians couldn't place it as anything they'd seen before. Have you had surgery abroad at any time?"

Bein jumped in to answer before Aoife could. They had to be careful now. They had no idea what they were dealing with and didn't want to alert the doctor to anything being amiss.

"Debbie broke her leg when we backpacked through Europe but that was years ago. It was a clean break so I have no idea why they would've put an implant in there."

He looked at Aoife hoping like hell she could read his cue.

Aoife turned to the doctor. "Can I have it taken out now?"

The man shook his head and he saw the edge of fear creep into Aoife's cheeks and squeezed her hand in support.

"I'm afraid you'll need to see your GP about that. It's not something we do here in accident and emergency."

"Oh."

Bein didn't want to call in favours and draw attention to himself, but they needed that chip or whatever the hell it was out of her leg this second. God knew how much time they had before Doyle found them now.

"Is Dr Goodwin still working in this department?" Bein knew he was. He also knew he was head of the department now.

"Yes, he is."

"Is he working today?"

"I believe so."

It was like pulling teeth, having a conversation with this man. "Can I please speak to him?"

"I'll see if he's free."

"Thank you." Bein didn't like acting like a dick to get his way, but in this case, it was warranted.

When they were alone Aoife leaned into him, her eyes searching his. "Bram?"

"It's going to be okay, Irish." He held her hand tight, his senses alert as he typed out a quick text to give Snow and Titan the heads up.

"This is why, isn't it? This is how he always finds me."

"Let's talk when we get home." He glanced up at the ceiling and the cameras, warning her that everything was being recorded and although he knew Watchdog had everything in place to remove footage of him, it might take time to remove Aoife. The case with Duchess was moving quicker than they'd anticipated, and Watchdog was juggling that as well as this situation.

The curtain was once again pulled back and he was being pulled into Dr Goodwin's arms and slapped hard on the back.

Marcus Goodwin pulled back to look at him with a grin, his smiling face a blast from the past. "Well, I never. The prodigal son returns."

"Marcus, it's so good to see you."

"You too, Bram. What is it, ten years?"

"Almost," Bram agreed.

Marcus had been one of the men who'd seen him beat Ray Walsh and his silence and loyalty had helped save him.

"Life good?"

Bein knew Marcus was asking him if he was okay. Each one of his friends had tried to reach out but due to the agreement with Jack, it had been hard for a while. Only after a few years had Jack agreed it was safe to make minimal contact. "Yes, life is very good. You?"

"Fantastic. I drive a Porsche and have a job I love. What more could a man need?"

"I'm glad, man. Listen, I hate to be that person, but I have a favour to ask. My girl has an implant in her leg, and we need it taken out, like now."

Marcus turned to Aoife and smiled his lady killer grin. "Nice to meet you, Debbie. Bram always did have fantastic taste."

Bein could feel himself cringe inside when he thought about his youth and the way he treated women. "Yeah, that's in the past."

"Understood. Now let's have a look."

Marcus held the X-ray to the light and frowned before he lowered it. "Should be simple enough as it's not deep. I can give you a local anaesthetic and remove it now."

"Thanks, Marcus. I appreciate that."

"No problem."

His old friend slipped into his role of doctor, one which he'd wanted since he was a boy and got to work. Aoife didn't even flinch when the needle went in, he was the one that looked away when Marcus made the small cut and removed the chip. Marcus popped it into a little test tube and glued the wound closed before putting a small dressing over it.

"There you go, all done."

Bein shook his hand. "Thank you, friend."

"My pleasure, and it was nice to meet you, Debbie. Make sure you keep this one on his toes."

Aoife beamed and you had to be dead not to feel the effects of her smile. "I will and thank you again."

"No problem. Don't be a stranger, Bram."

"I won't."

Bein knew that was a lie. Not because he didn't want to stay in touch but because he couldn't, and he sensed Marcus knew it.

Marcus drew the curtain as he left, and Bein helped Aoife pull her joggers up to cover herself.

"Ready to get out of here?"

"Hell yes."

Bein pocketed the test tube, knowing they'd need to analyse everything they could to find out where they stood and how much information Doyle had received.

Snow and Titan met him at the exit and flanked them as they walked to the car with Aoife moving slower because of her crutches. That she used them so proficiently made him furious. The only way a person was an expert with crutches was if they'd used them a lot, and he knew the reason she had was her evil father.

When he got his hands on him, there'd be no mercy. Men like him didn't deserve it. He'd thought long and hard about what Titan had said and he was at peace with ending her father's life to free Aoife from his hold.

When they got back to the castle, he helped Aoife up to the room they were now sharing and settled her on the bed. He left Lana and Mrs Murrel fussing over her and with a kiss on her head, went to brief his team.

The small, dream-like respite they'd had was over and instead of hiding, he wanted them to go on the offensive and hunt Doyle down. Snow and Titan were waiting for him in his father's old office which still had the lingering scent of cigar smoke. This time though, it didn't cause him upset but made him more resolute in what he had to do. It was time to be Bein, not Bram.

CHAPTER 23

Bram pulled away from the kiss with Aoife knowing that if he continued, he wouldn't leave. He was loathe to leave her already, but he had no choice, the team needed to meet face to face and have a proper plan in place to end Doyle. He knew from the information he had that Doyle was safely in Ireland and the castle was protected.

Rory had assured him he wouldn't leave Aoife unprotected and Bram trusted him with his life and the lives of those he loved. After all, nobody loved harder than Rory and Lana.

"I need to go or I'll crawl back into bed with you."

It was early, only four in the morning, and the cover of darkness would work in everyone's favour for the four-hour journey.

"Be safe, Bram."

"Just say inside the castle."

Aoife lifted her leg tempting him and he let his hand run over the silky skin. "As if I can do much else."

He'd learned over the last twenty-four hours that Aoife didn't like being cooped up and was a terrible patient. "It's a good job you're sexy because you're a pain in the arse as a patient."

Aoife huffed but he could see her smile in the light from the fire. "Be gone. Stop bothering me and go be manly and save the world."

Bram left, taking the stairs silently to meet Snow and Titan at the back door.

Rory was waiting with them, and Bram shook his hand. "Thanks, brother."

"We're family, Bram, that's what we do."

Bram tipped his head and the three of them headed for the Range Rover. Titan would drive them to a rendezvous point on the English border and a known safehouse they used where the others would meet them.

Duchess was still in London with Reaper and Bishop working on the Cavendish brothers but Watchdog, Bás, Hurricane, and Lotus would be there. Apparently, Lotus was also bringing Rykov Anatolievich with her, who'd agreed to help them.

Bram didn't know him well but after hearing how close Hurricane had come to getting captured in Ireland a few weeks earlier, he was happy to take all the help they could get to end this once and for all.

Doyle clearly had more people loyal to him than they knew of, but what he wasn't sure of was whether it was adoration or fear which fuelled their loyalty, and the difference could be huge for how they proceeded.

The motorways were clear this early as they pulled off and waited at a service station for the allotted time to make sure they were clear of a tail. Titan pulled back on the road and continued until they hit Berwick-upon-Tweed, a small town of about twelve thousand people on the east coast. Pulling into a family suburb where people were just getting ready for the workday, Bram, Snow, and Titan headed inside, knowing from the text that Bás and the others were already waiting for them.

Straightening his spine for whatever was to come, he shucked off the cloak of Bram and allowed Bein to take over.

The dining room had been set up like a conference room, the

windows on the unassuming house were bullet proof so they had no concerns about that as they sat around the table and waited for Bás to speak.

"Firstly, how is Aoife?"

He had to stop the sappy look he could feel edging over his features at the thought of her. "Fine. She took a tumble in the woods and fractured her metatarsal, but it turned out to be a good thing. Without it, we would've been chasing our tails looking for a leak that never was."

Bás linked his fingers together on the table. "Yes, and because of that, we've cleared Peyton. She's staying with Smithy and Lizzie until this is over. I think being stuck unable to see her patients was taking a toll on her. Now, back to business. Hurricane, do you have an update for us on what you learned in Ireland?"

Bein glanced around the room at his friends and noticed Rykov watching Lotus. It was no secret to anyone how he felt about Lotus, but she wouldn't have any of it. He also knew she was the reason he was helping them out and he'd take it.

"His operation is bigger than we realised. He owns that city. Nobody gets in or out without him knowing about it. He owns The Smugglers Rest pub in Dublin and it's his main haunt. He spends some time at his home which is guarded twenty-four-seven, but he's mainly at the pub. He's there every night and surrounded by guards, all armed, but it's not them that concern me, it's all the others. He seems to control everyone, from the shop owners to the homeless guy who lives in the alley. It's like his own network, which is why nobody can get near him. I was minutes from getting caught when I got on that flight out. Another fifteen minutes and he would've had me."

"Did you learn anything about the operation?" Rykov asked, his accent thick.

Hurricane shrugged. "We know he runs the docks and from the access he has to the airfield, my guess is he has people from customs and security at the airport on his payroll. It's so dirty, it's hard to see where his stink doesn't touch. He has judges, cops, officials of every kind on his books or he has dirt on them. I also think he uses a double sometimes." Hurricane sipped his cold coffee and grimaced before he continued. "So basically, un-fucking-touchable."

Bein could feel his frustration growing with every second and revelation.

"Not necessarily." All eyes turned to Rykov who had unbuttoned the jacket of his bespoke handmade suit and leaned forward. "I've spoken with my contact in the US and I'm expecting a call from Igor Popov later today. I'm going to offer him a deal he won't refuse to walk away from his deal with Doyle. If you take Doyle and his closest men from the equation, then I have people who can take over his territory."

Bein felt his lip curl in disgust. "Are you fucking with me? You want us to take out Doyle, so you slip in and take over his drug trade?"

Rykov regarded him silently for a minute. "Yes. Doyle is an unknown and out of control element but what I'm proposing isn't the Bratva taking over, but the Diablo Riders."

"Excuse me, but you want a biker gang to take over and you think it will be better?" Bein clenched his fists on the table, his feelings on this mirrored around the room.

"Yes, I do. Diablos are all made up of ex-military. They run drugs and guns but don't touch sex trafficking or tolerate abuse of women. They also have the knowledge and manpower to handle this coup when Doyle goes down."

"So why haven't they?" Bás asked the question they were all now thinking.

"Because with Doyle alive people are too scared to back them. He has everyone in that city afraid. He doesn't just run his personal life with fear, he runs the entire town. You either do what he says or suffer, and he's cruel."

Bein snorted. "You don't need to tell us that. He did hideous things to his own child and allowed his men to torture and abuse her."

Bein saw the sympathy and while he didn't know Rykov's story, he saw the anger and passion with which he'd defend women against crime. "I'm aware, which is why he needs to die."

"I'm still not sure an MC gang taking over will leave the city better off," Titan began, his own history as a gang leader making him the best person to weigh in on this.

"I understand that, but you and I both know if you leave nothing in place the void will be filled by someone. At least this way we control the narrative and I have assurances from the president of the club that they will be fair and clean up the city."

"Let me speak to my contact in Ireland before we approve that, but I agree our only plan is to take out Doyle." Bás pointed at Watch-dog, aka Jonas Mason, who as usual had his head buried in his screen. He was the kind of man who never seemed to be off, always working either on his screen or in the gym. For that reason, he was as far away from what anyone would expect a geek to look like as they could get but without a doubt, he was the best.

"I want a weakness. Find me a way in so I can take down Doyle and weaken him."

"You know the quickest way is to draw him out."

Bein glared at Lotus knowing exactly what she was suggesting. He pointed his finger her way. "No fucking way."

Lotus, never one to back down, was determined though. "I know you care about her, Bein, but we both know in any other situation you would've suggested it already."

He knew she was right, but this wasn't some random person, it was the woman he was in love with. "I said no."

Bás waved his hand impatiently to silence them. "Shut the fuck up. I can't think. Titan, do you agree with the MC taking over?"

"I'd need to know more about them before I comment but I agree with what Rykov says about a void. If you leave one, it will be filled by someone."

"Rykov, are you vouching for these people?"

"I will on my honour."

"Good because if this goes south, you're the person I'm coming for."

"Understood."

"Handle Popov and have these men ready to move."

Bás looked at him. "Word is Doyle put out a reward for any information on Aoife. That just upped our timeline. We know he has men still loyal to him and his right-hand man, Conlan O'Neill, never leaves his side. We also know O'Neill has some pretty disgusting tastes that run to barely legal girls or boys. Speak to Aoife and see if she can remember anything else that might help us. We know we can't get close to him physically, but we might need to consider luring him to us."

Bein shoved the chair back as he stood abruptly, slamming his hands down on the table. "I fucking said no."

"Not your call, Bein. This is bigger than you or Aoife now. We can't allow a man like him to continue running one of the biggest cities in Ireland. It's a threat to national security and you know it."

"There must be another way."

"Like?"

Bein was glaring at his boss, fear wrapping around the edge of his throat and cutting off his air. He couldn't risk Doyle getting near Aoife again. "What if I meet with him? If I can get close enough, I can kill him."

"That's fucking suicide."

Bein remained silent, he knew it was, but he'd rather do that than risk Aoife.

Bás was looking at him in shock. "You really ready to die for this girl?"

"Yes."

Three little letters but they meant more than any declaration of love. If it meant she lived free he'd happily take his chances.

"No, I won't lose one of my men to insanity for pussy."

Bein didn't know what happened, but he had Bás across the table before anyone could move. His hand around his throat, tight as his vision swam red with rage. "Never fucking call her that again."

Bás didn't fucking blink, the man never even made a sound. Everyone around them was moving and shouting but they seemed to have an unspoken conversation before Hurricane and Titan grabbed him and pulled him away.

"What the fuck are you thinking, Bein?"

Lotus punched him in the face hard, waking him from his rage-filled trance. His cheek throbbed as he pulled out of Titan's grip. "Get the fuck off me."

Titan still had a hold of his arm. "You good?"

"Yeah." He shook off the hold and walked through the kitchen.

He needed fresh air, his lungs burning, his head swimming. He felt like he was losing control with everything spiralling. How had he gone from calm and rational to attacking his boss and the man who had done so much for him?

Sitting on the step of the back door overlooking the coastline he shoved his hands in his hair. It was like Ray Walsh all over again.

He felt a presence beside him and turned to find Snow sitting beside him, silently watching the horizon. "When I was small, I used to believe that monsters were real. My dad told me the real monsters were in our heads. That we were the ones who gave them control and allowed them to take up residence for free and rule."

He glanced across at her. "Did you believe him?"

"Yes and no. We both know doing this job that monsters and evil are real. It's why we do what we do, but I think he made some sense. Which is whacked considering he was drunk most of the time. I think we allow things we see and do to affect us more than we should. Oh, I know it's easy to say that, and keeping the demons at bay is hard, especially for us. Those that live with one foot either side of the fence, never quite knowing if we're the monster or the hero, but if we don't fight the monsters then they win."

Snow turned to him, knocking his shoulder with her own. "Aoife sees the hero in you and for that reason, you have to fight the monster. Be the man she loves, the man your sister and family loves. Bás was pushing you and you let him. I get why you want to confront Doyle, but if you do that, you condemn Aoife to a life knowing she's the reason you died."

"But she isn't responsible for his actions."

"No, she isn't. Only he is, but we all insist on carrying guilt for things we didn't do or couldn't control. It's human nature and I'm sure you know that better than anyone."

He knew exactly what she was saying and for the first time in his life, he understood what she meant. He couldn't let Aoife carry that guilt that had weighed so heavy for him with Lana. He had to find another way. "You're pretty astute for a Frenchie."

Snow arched her brow at him. "And you're not so dumb for a Jock."

"Touché. Thanks, Snow."

"Anytime, Bein." She stood and held out a hand to him. "Now, I suggest you get back inside and apologise before Bás has you on guard duty for the rest of your natural-born life."

That didn't bother him, he'd take his punishment like a man, but she was right, he did owe him an apology and an explanation.

Bás was nursing a cup of coffee in the living room and looked up as he walked in and sat in the opposite chair. "I'm sorry. I was out of line and there's no excuse for it."

Bás remained silent for a moment before he sat forward and placed his cup on the glass coffee table. "You love her."

"Yes, I do."

"I didn't know."

"I only just figured it out myself."

"Listen, I get why you offered but I can't allow you to sacrifice yourself. It would be too big of a loss both to the team and on a personal level. You know how this works. We aren't just a team, we're family, and you'd no more let me do it than I'd let you. I get you want to protect her, but this isn't the way. We'll find another way to take him down."

"He needs to die, Bás."

"I know and he will. But you don't get to die with him."

"I know, Snow read me the riot act in the way only she can."

"How has she seemed to you?"

Bein frowned. "Who? Snow?"

"Yes."

"Fine, why?"

"Something's going on with her and when this is over, I need to find out what it is."

Bein stayed quiet but knew he'd be watching his friend closer now.

"We good, boss?"

Bás took the hand Bein offered. "We're good but you pull a stunt like that again we're going to have a problem."

"Understood. It won't happen again."

"You're a good man, Bein. Flawed like the rest of us but inside where it counts your heart is good. You just need to remember that."

Bein felt the tension leave him knowing that his boss, and more importantly his friends, had his back.

His phone ringing in his pocket made him turn to the window as she answered his sister's call.

His blood ran cold at the first tear-filled words out of her mouth.

"Bram, oh God. I'm so sorry. We couldn't stop him."

CHAPTER 24

Ten long years he'd been waiting for his revenge and now it was within his grasp. It should've been harder but with a face so familiar around the village that it blended in; it had been easy to gain access to the castle. Now all he needed to do was carry out his plan and history would be avenged.

He'd watched them all these weeks, planning and plotting, altering his appearance so nobody would recognise him and now it was time to act. He'd seen them leave under cover of darkness thinking they were clever, that the people they loved were safe, but fate had been on his side.

Now not only would he get revenge on the whore who'd caused this but also the man who'd ruined his family and taken his brother's life and gotten away with it. They all thought he was free and clear, that justice wasn't meant for them, but he was there to deliver it.

Cutting through the back stairs used by the servants, he turned the corner his usual disguise gone, and stopped dead at the site of Mrs Murrel. The old bat was there earlier than planned.

"Boyd, what are you doing here?"

She stepped back, knowing he had no reason to be in the castle and the family history between him and the McCullums was anything but sweetness and light.

He moved toward her, and she turned to run, her big fat trap open ready to give the game away, but he couldn't allow her to ruin his plans, not when everything was finally going his way and his ticket out of this God-forsaken shit hole was within reach.

Grabbing a vase from the side table, he swung and the old bat fell forward, her scream dying in her throat as she hit the ground, the vase by some miracle still intact in his hands. Even fate was on his side today it seemed. Bending, he saw blood pooling on the ground and wondered if she was dead. He didn't care. What was one more death in this war? Either way, she was silent now and his plan was in play.

He left her slumped where she was and rushed up the stairs. He had no time to drag her into the pantry, he needed to move and someone finding her was a risk he had to take. Taking the stairs two at a time now, he avoided the creaky floorboards which he'd taken painstaking weeks learning as he hoovered this goddamn dust trap. Keeping his head down like a good little soldier and doing the work, and now it was time for the pay-off. Arriving on the landing of the second floor unheard was his reward for bowing and scraping to these assholes.

Rory, the fake lord of the manor, had left to work in his office on the ground floor after Bram and his weird friends left but Boyd wasn't stupid. No, he'd looped the camera feed so it showed what he wanted him to see which was nothing but divine peace. He knew it was only a matter of time though before the house started to wake, especially with the brats getting ready for school.

Putting his ear to the door where he knew the woman slept, Boyd listened, his hands sweating, his pulse racing with excitement and adrenaline. Opening the door, he winced at the creak he couldn't avoid and stepped inside. Seeing her asleep in the huge bed, assured by her murdering boyfriend that she was safe when safety was an illusion, made him smile with excitement. Closing the heavy door behind him he tiptoed to the bed.

She looked like an angel, and he could see why so many men wanted to get their hands on her. She was perfect, her pouty lips inviting even in sleep, her body made for the seduction and destruction of men. Skin so pale it gave her fragility that seemed to call to the beast in him.

Leaning closer, he could smell the scent of her body, intoxicating and sweet, mixed with sex and desire. He felt his own body tighten with the flood of lust but looked away, tamping it down. Weeks of watching her had gotten to him, but this wasn't his mission. He wouldn't allow a beautiful face to destroy his mission. He needed to remember why he was there and not allow this witch to sway his mind.

Slamming his hand over her mouth, he watched with a feeling of immense power as her eyes snapped open and blind fear almost choked her. She began to struggle, and he held the gun in his free hand up so she could see it. Her eyes moved over it, tears filling her green eyes, making them seem luminous and bright like a jewel.

"Silence or everyone in this castle dies. Do you understand me?"

Aoife nodded. She was a clever one, catching on quick to who had the true power here.

"Good, now get up slowly and don't make a sound or those little brats are going to die a horrible death."

Aoife moved slowly, swinging her legs out of the bed, her body covered by tartan pyjamas. As soon as she was standing, he turned her, looping her arms together and tying them with rope. He gagged her mouth so she couldn't scream and bent, his gun still on her and slipped her feet into slippers. He wasn't an animal after all, and she was a means to an end and not the real enemy.

"Now, we're going to go out the secret tunnel in here and nobody gets hurt."

He moved to the window where he knew the entrance to the

tunnel was hidden, just as the door swung open and the smile on Lana's face died at the sight of him.

"Get in here and don't make a fucking sound or this bitch dies."

"W... why are you doing this?" Her skin was pale as she moved to close the door, her eyes seeking out Aoife and an escape as she did.

"Isn't it obvious, Lana? You and Bram took something from me and now I'm going to take something from you. You should be glad it isn't one of those brats in here instead of her. Luckily for you, this does the job, and I get a huge payday from her loving father." The hand he had on Aoife felt the tension radiate through her at the mention of her father.

"You mean Ray?"

"Yes, of course I mean Ray. That animal murdered my brother in cold blood and never got punished, so now I'm here to remedy that."

"Ray raped me, Boyd. He raped me and laughed about it."

"You taunted him, you led him on for weeks in your slutty clothes. He told me how much you wanted it."

"I said no. He raped me." Lana was standing taller now, her conviction confusing him, making him doubt the truth but he knew what she was doing. She was trying to confuse him, to make him doubt his brother's character.

"Stop, I won't let you lie to me. Bram killed him because he was jealous, and he got away with it. Now I'm going to make sure he hurts just like I have for the last ten years."

"Listen, Boyd, you don't need to do this."

"I do and you need to shut up or I'm going to put a bullet in your belly and kill the brat you're carrying. Let your kids find you dead in a pool of your own blood like I watched my brother be beaten to death."

He saw sympathy in her eyes, and it made him angrier. How dare she pity him. He knew he couldn't take her with him too, much as he wanted to but he could only cover tracks for one of them, and this one would be quicker despite her injury.

"Here, gag yourself with this." He threw a scarf at her and

watched her pick it up and secure it over her mouth. "Now sit on the floor and if you try and run, she dies."

With his eyes and gun trained on Aoife, he tied Lana's legs and feet and dragged her to the other side of the bed.

Through tear-filled eyes she watched her, her eyes begging him to relent, to leave. He could see why his brother had wanted her. Lana was beautiful with a regal grace that drew men to her.

Turning his back on her, he grabbed Aoife by the arm and pulled. She whimpered as she fell into him, putting her against his hardness and making him feel powerful.

"Let's go."

Boyd pushed on the panel that opened the tunnel door and, using the flashlight on his phone, peered inside. Satisfied it was clear, he shoved Aoife in first and, with one last look at Lana, the cause of all his pain, he left. He would've liked to have stayed and spent some time showing her just how much hurt she'd caused him with her lies but he couldn't, and Bram was the real target.

He'd been the one to murder Ray, to end his life. He was the one who deserved every inch of pain coming his way. He got to watch Aoife being handed over to her father, who from a few searches he'd done, Boyd knew was the devil personified. Regret tinged him that she'd suffer, but that was of no concern to him. He just wanted revenge on Bram and the huge fucking payday so he could restart his life somewhere else with a clean slate. Maybe he could go to Mexico and spend his days on the beach with women doing his bidding.

But first, Bram needed to die at his hand and suffer for every punch he'd ever inflicted on Ray, and for leaving him without his adored brother to grow up in that hell that was his family life.

As the tunnel wound lower, Aoife lost her footing a couple of times and he had to grab her.

"Stop fucking messing around. Or do I need to remind you what I'll do to Lana and her brats if they catch up to us?"

Aoife shook her head and managed to make it the rest of the way without slipping or stumbling. As they got outside, he pushed her roughly behind him, not wanting to give her a chance to run. He listened intently to the silence outside, waiting to catch a hint that the alarm had been raised but heard nothing but blessed silence.

Satisfied that his luck was still running, he pushed open the door and dragged Aoife into the early morning darkness. The cold hit him like a whip as the rain lashed the land and the wind blew the frigid cold across his skin.

"Move."

With his hand wrapped tight around Aoife's upper arm, he yanked her towards the edge of the estate lawn and into the cut-through that led to the woods. The gravel and grass would hide his tracks with the help of the rain but the deeper they moved into the woods, the more careful he needed to be to make sure they couldn't be easily followed.

He knew Bram was an expert tracker, but he was better. He'd been working towards this for years, making his plans, learning the land. He knew every tree or curve like his own face.

Finally, after what seemed like hours, he reached the place he'd set up for them to wait until Doyle came through.

Dragging a shivering Aoife into the cave, he pushed her down onto the sleeping bags he'd been using for the past few days as he slept in this cold hell, waiting for the perfect moment. He'd known with patience it would present itself and it had.

"Here, this should warm you up." The rain had soaked through her nightclothes, soaking her to the bone. She shivered so hard he worried she might pass out. Boyd draped a fur blanket around her shoulders, and she looked at him with gratitude but remained silent, her mouth still gagged.

He needed to make a phone call and then he could untie the gag and feed her. He didn't need his golden goose dead before she could get him the cash to change his life.

Stepping to the edge of the narrow cave, Boyd hit dial on the number he'd been given for Doyle. After two rings it was picked up.

"Boyd, what do you have for me?"

He didn't like dealing with Conlan, the man was evil personified, even more so than Doyle and that was saying something. Conlan was creepy and killed for fun. At least with Doyle, it was merely business.

"Get Doyle to call me back in two minutes. I have his daughter." Boyd hung up, his hand shaking slightly.

Moments later his phone rang, and he tried not to smile in triumph.

"Boyd, where is my daughter?"

"Mr Doyle, she's here with me and safe. I'll give you her location in twenty-four hours when I'm sure the money has been transferred."

Doyle laughed. "Now, why would I take orders off a little prick like you?"

"Because if you do, I'll also give you the location of the man who took her from you and killed your men."

"I'm listening."

"Transfer my money and in twenty-four hours, you'll have the location."

Boyd hung up knowing he'd either just made a huge mistake with a powerful enemy, or he'd secured his place as a man to be reckoned with.

CHAPTER 25

"Bram, oh God. I'm so sorry. We couldn't stop him."

His hand tightened on the phone and, sensing the tension, Bás stepped forward. "Calm down, Lana, and tell me what happened."

He heard the hiccup down the line and had to stop himself from losing his mind and bellowing at his sister to tell him what happened.

"Boyd Walsh. He broke into the house after you left and kidnapped Aoife from her bed."

His skin felt like it was being flayed alive as fear sent electric pulses through his body. As calmly as he could, he placed the phone on the table and put the call on speaker. He needed his team in on this and explaining twice would take more time than he wanted. "Is everyone okay?"

Lana began to cry and the next voice he heard was Rory's.

"Bram, I'm so sorry. He hurt Mrs Murrel. She's on her way to the hospital with a blunt force head trauma."

Bram closed his eyes thinking of the woman who was more of a grandmother to him than a staff member. "What about Lana?"

"She's shaken. He tied her up and gagged her in Aoife's room. I found her after I found Mrs Murrel. The police are here too and want a statement. What should I say?"

"Just tell them what happened but leave my team out of it. We're on our way back now and will fix this." He took a breath. "Do the cameras show how he got out and which way he went?"

Bram could see the rest of the team gathering and listening intently as Watchdog began to type, already hunting for Boyd Walsh.

"He took her through the inner tunnel, but he looped the camera inside so it wouldn't show him. It seems he has a good knowledge of the house, but I did find a set of prints on the lawn when I had a quick look once I realised which way he'd gone."

"Okay, we start there. I'll be home in a few hours, and we'll begin looking. Don't let the police know which way they went if there are tracks. I don't want them trampling all over them."

"I'll tell them he went out the front so they'll concentrate on the roads."

"Good and get a team of the best trackers in the village assembled at the castle."

"You think he took her into the woods?"

"I think if Boyd has been planning revenge for this long, he knows not to take the roads. The cops can check them and so can my team, but nobody knows the woods better than us, and I know if I was doing this, then that's where I'd take her. Take care of Lana and the kids until I get there and tell her I love her."

"Will do, Bram."

Bram cut the call. Everyone was silent while they gathered up their equipment and, in minutes, headed to the cars and were on their way. He was in a car with Titan, Snow, and Bás riding shotgun, as the rest of the team followed in the vehicles they'd driven up in.

Bram looked at Bás, who he knew was waiting for an explanation and more details and appreciated the fact the team had jumped into action without knowing the full story. "Boyd is the younger brother of a man named Ray Walsh. Ray raped my sister when she was eighteen and I beat him to death. I had no idea his brother was harbouring a grudge or that he even knew I was home but it seems I fucked up because he somehow broke into the castle after we left and took Aoife."

"I'll have Watchdog look into him and find out all we can about the man. I heard you tell Rory to get some trackers together. Why?"

"Boyd took Aoife out through a secret tunnel inside the walls of the castle that only the family knows about. That shows he knows the castle well and has been inside for an extended period. It also shows a level of cunning, and a man who's waited this long for revenge isn't going to fuck it up by using the main road to get her out when everyone in the village knows his face. My guess is he'll take her deeper into the estate."

"That's good, right? It's your land and you know it better than anyone."

"Yes and no. I know it like the back of my hand but at this time of the year in the cold and rain, Aoife is at serious risk of exposure."

"Yeah, and that land ain't small, boss. I went out with Rory a few times. It's vast and spread over miles and miles."

Bram glanced at Titan who was driving, his foot to the floor to get them home. "He's right but if I can track him, I can figure out where he might go."

"Will Rory keep his mouth shut?"

"Yeah, we can trust him." Bram knew his brother-in-law would be feeling sick about this, but it wasn't his fault. No, once again the fault lay with him, he was the reason Boyd had come after Aoife. It was payback for killing his older brother. He tried to remember Boyd but only got the sense of a younger brother who followed Ray around like a puppy. He was probably in his early twenties at most and most likely had grown up with a false sense of who his brother was. "Rory adores my sister. I mean worships the ground she walks on, and his kids are his life. So, yes, we can trust him."

Bram looked out of the window, fighting the bloodthirst pounding through his body to find Boyd and kill him for ever laying a finger on Aoife, the other part of him was filled with pure terror that he wouldn't find her in time. That he'd get to her, and she'd be hurt or worse and he would've failed again, to protect the person he loved. And he did love her, he knew that without a second's doubt.

The thought of her cold or in pain, frightened or scared slayed him and he had to clench his fists to stop from lashing out in impotent anger. No, he needed to rein in the rage, to do what the army and Shadow had taught him and use it, control it, and turn it into what he needed to find Aoife and get her back.

Bás' phone rang, and he answered it briskly on the first ring. Bram continued looking at his own phone as Rory sent him updates that he had three men he trusted with his life to help them, and he'd sent Lana and the kids to stay with his mother and father. That was good, the last thing they needed was the kids or Lana getting hurt any more than she had already.

"Fuck."

Bram looked sharply at Bás. "What is it?"

"That was Watchdog. He said a wire transfer for five hundred thousand pounds was just made into Boyd's account from an account that traces back to Doyle."

Bram felt the colour drain from him at the thought of his worlds colliding and Aoife now being at the mercy of not only his enemy but also her father. "Boyd must have seen the reward, which proves the lowlife circles he's moving in."

"True and that's not all. Doyle just chartered a flight from Dublin to London Gatwick, which means he's on the move."

Bram frowned. "Why Gatwick?"

"Maybe he doesn't know where Aoife is yet. If Boyd is clever, which it seems he might be, then he won't give Doyle the location without proof of the money in his account."

Bram shook his head. "Doyle wouldn't fall for that. He wouldn't let Boyd call the shots like that. Unless Boyd is offering more than just Aoife."

"He's giving them us, too. But how would he know that we're involved?"

"He won't, but he knows I'm with Aoife and offering up the man she's with would seem like a good way for revenge and a pay-out. Boyd gets the cash and hands me over to Doyle, who'll dish out the punishment."

"Maybe, it doesn't all make sense yet, but I do believe we're on the right track." Bás glanced back to Snow who had been quiet so far. "Snow, anything to add?"

"How did he know about the tunnels?"

Bram shrugged, he really had no idea, as far as he knew only family knew of them. "That I don't know."

"You need to check your staff and find out if anyone didn't turn up today. My guess is he's been under your nose the entire time, hiding in plain sight."

"You think? That's brazen."

"It is but also the best approach a lot of times. People ignore things they see all the time to the point they become invisible."

"Good point."

Bram called Rory who promised to take a look and speak with the main staff members straight away, and also gave him an update. He also told him that Mrs Murrel was in surgery, and he'd keep him updated before hanging up.

"This is all my fault."

"Bullshit. This is Boyd's fault and Doyle's fault, not yours."

Bram glared at Snow who'd turned in her seat to face him, her normally sweet smile gone, replaced by determination, which was bone-deep. "I murdered his brother."

"Who raped Lana. You did what any of us would've done." Titan was looking at him in the rear-view mirror as he spoke.

"Would you have killed him?"

"Without a shadow of a doubt, I would have. I did much worse to avenge my brothers. I know I'm not that man anymore but I'm not sure I'd do that part differently if I had the chance. We aren't choir boys, Bein. We're not the heroes. We fight the good fight, but we fight it dirty and raw and yes, we break the law, and many would say our morals are skewed but the truth is they need us to be those people. The world needs the grey we provide when the system lets them down. That's why we exist, why Jack set up this team with the approval from the highest word in the land."

"It was long-winded and wordy, but Titan is right. We are what we are." Snow smirked at Titan as she squeezed Bram's arm in support.

Perhaps his friends were right and he was taking on blame that should belong to someone else, but a lifetime of service was ingrained to be better, and maybe he couldn't see that his better was just different to others.

"Okay, now all the kumbaya shit is out the way, we need a strategy to protect our backs from Doyle and find Aoife. I propose Watchdog, Lotus, Rykov, who for some reason is coming with us, set up the castle and scope the place as a stronghold. If Doyle gets there before we find Aoife... We need to make sure he doesn't find her first and also protect the villagers. He won't think twice about killing them all and starting an all-out war."

"The castle was built to protect Laird and Lady McCullum from the English, and it's a very defensive position," Titan added.

"We can set up tripwires on the perimeter and have Watchdog handle the surveillance. We have enough weapons in the boot and I can get Rory to make sure the gun cupboard is available. I wish we had Valentina, Monty, and Scout with us. They'd certainly help us find Aoife quicker." Bein could feel the tension and worry eating at him.

"Yeah, me too, but she's visiting Rafe and his girl Nix in Oxford for a few days. I can ask Bás to call her in, but my guess is by the time she gets up here you'll have already found her." Titan agreed.

"Yeah, leave it. We have enough people to find Aoife. You just worry about Doyle."

"Let me handle that. You find Aoife so we have the upper hand with that at least. I'll oversee everything when we get there. You just find your girl and deal with Boyd."

"I'll find the little bastard and when I do, he's going to wish he never heard my name."

The rest of the journey was Bás on the phone making plans and giving orders, doing what he did best, while Bram sat and thought about the different spots he'd go to if he was trying to hide out in the woods and mentally narrowed it down to three possible locations. He'd need to speak to Rory first though and get his opinion. He knew the estate better than him these days and he valued his brother-in-law's thoughts. How was he ever going to make this up to Aoife? He'd beg her to forgive him, because selfish bastard that he was, he knew after this he couldn't give her up and walk away from her no matter how much he should.

She was his heart and she belonged with him if she'd have him.

CHAPTER 26

Aoife had been feigning sleep for the last twenty minutes or so as she watched the man who had taken her pace the entrance to the cave where he had her captive. Boyd, that was what Lana had called him and she mentioned his brother had raped her.

Aoife felt her heart break for the woman she'd come to care for in the last few weeks. Sympathy and empathy for the pain and feelings of shame and guilt that she knew from bitter experience came with an attack like that. It was the worst violation a person could go through and that it'd happened to someone else she knew made her angry, fury ripping through her veins.

Yet it was the other things he said that were forefront in her mind right this second. Boyd kept saying how Bram had murdered his brother. Was that in retribution for raping his sister? She didn't know but she did know it was part of the reason that Bram probably thought he was a bad person, that he had a darkness inside of him.

She didn't see it that way, if he'd done what Boyd said then she felt nothing but pride for the man who had defended his sister. Was it right to kill? No, she knew that, but neither was rape or child abuse or a hundred other things and yet animals who thought themselves human got away with it every day on technicalities or because the victim was treated like the criminal.

Perhaps it made her a bad person, but she felt only pride and love for a man who would defend those he loved with such conviction. She'd seen him with his nieces and nephews, and they adored him and the feeling she knew was mutual. How could a man who would let a child paint his nails for a tea party be evil? To her mind, he wasn't, and she'd never believe otherwise.

Her leg cramped up, the pain of the cold in her limbs, which were giving her pins and needles as they warmed up, making her flinch. Boyd looked at her sharply and pointed his tall frame moving closer.

"You're my payback."

Aoife understood he wanted her to ask why so he could tell her all the ways she'd suffer and frighten her but she was immune to such things. When someone lived with evil every day they became accustomed to it as if the dark veiled threats became a part of them. She wanted to know more about his brother and what Bram had done though, so she'd play his game. It would pass the time while she waited for Bram to find her, and she had no doubt he would.

The bracelet she'd dropped on their way through the woods would hopefully be found and he'd save her. It was the first time since her mother had died that she had hope and she'd hold onto it until her dying breath. "What for?"

Boyd swung from the pacing he was doing at the edge of the cave. The rain had eased but the cold hadn't let up, the fog not lifting an inch since they'd hit the tree line. She didn't know what time it was, but her guess was it had to be somewhere around nine am.

"What for? How can you lie with a man and not know who he is, what he has done?" Boyd moved closer to her his finger pointed in accusation at her. He was tall with blond hair, which was almost the same colour as his skin, making him look boring and nondescript. He wasn't ugly, but he was forgettable. His build was average, but she knew he was strong and he was probably of average height. Even his eyes held nothing but grey with no evil or warmth, he was just nothing.

"Bram is a good man. He loves his family and he loves me."

"He doesn't know what it is to love someone, or he'd never have done what he did."

"Bram knows better than anyone what love is. I know evil and he's not it."

"Your father?"

"Yes."

"He's going to make me rich. He's paying me double for delivering you and Bram to him. I get rich and Bram will pay for his crimes."

"So, it's okay for someone to be hurt just as long as it's not someone you care about?"

Boyd sat on the edge of a rock, his hands moving through his hair, and she could see the struggle inside him. This man wasn't born evil, he'd become that way through grief and pain.

"My father allowed all his men to rape me. He'll kill me and Bram and you think that's okay?"

Boyd pulled at his hair, the strands coming out in chunks as his grip on things become less tangible. "He's a murderer."

Aoife titled her head "Your brother was a rapist."

Boyd's head shot up and he glared at her with hatred bordering on mania. "No, you do not say that. Ray wasn't what they say he was. He loved Lana and she led him on. She toyed with him." Spittle flew from his mouth as he began to pace again, and Aoife knew she should shut up and keep her head down.

"How much is my father paying you?"

"What?"

"How much is he paying you to hand me and Bram over to him?"

Boyd grinned, the money obviously making him happy, and she knew it had to be a lot.

"Five hundred grand for each of you and the promise that Bram will feel every ounce of the pain he inflicted on my brother."

Aoife shook her head. She knew her father would never pay that kind of money. Boyd was as good as dead. "You're a fool if you think he's going to pay you that. My father would never waste that much of his precious money on me."

Boyd grabbed her hair, dragging her close to his sneering face. Tears hit her eyes at the sting of pain in her scalp. "That's where you're wrong. Everyone thinks I'm stupid, that because I don't speak a lot, I'm dumb but I listen, and I learn. It's how I learned dear Bram and his little friends had killed his guards and pissed off your father even more. I knew then that was how I'd kill him. I'd leave it to the experts." His lip curled up in distaste. "I don't like killing, I'm not a murderer."

Aoife would almost feel sorry for this man if he didn't have her trussed up like a Christmas turkey, freezing her ass off in the middle of the Highlands in winter. "You will be if you hand me over to my father. He'll kill me and Bram. I know you think you're avenging your brother, but this isn't the way."

She knew appealing to his better nature was a long shot, he'd had years believing the things he did and letting his pain fester.

"Your father is paying five hundred grand upfront. I told him I'll contact him first thing tomorrow to give him the coordinates where he can find you."

"Is the money in your account yet?"

She'd never known her sperm donor to pay anyone upfront in her life, which meant he was serious about killing Bram and giving her to the Russian.

"I need to move up the hill to where I have signal and check."

Aoife remained silent. She knew Boyd was dead either way—be that from Bram or Doyle. He was too far gone to see the monster he'd become. Some would think her a hypocrite for believing Boyd was a monster and Bram a hero, but there was a big difference in her mind. Bram killed to defend the innocent and Boyd was using an innocent to satisfy his thirst for revenge.

Before he went, Boyd tightened the ropes on her wrists and

ankles and pulled the blanket tighter around her body. The cold was bone-deep now though, her teeth chattering hard, her fingers and toes numb, and she wondered if she slept if she'd wake up. Listening to Boyd walk away she wanted to call him back, but the gag had been replaced so she couldn't even call out.

Most of her life she'd been a positive person, a fighter, and since meeting Bram and getting to know Lana, Snow, Titan, and Rory she'd felt more like herself as they let her be who she was and not what they expected of her, and that person was a fighter. She was a woman who loved adventure and the outdoors, who wasn't afraid of getting her hands dirty finger painting with the kids.

She wasn't the weak little caricature of a perfect daughter her father had tried to make her. She didn't give a fuck if her nails weren't done, or her hair wasn't in sleek waves, or her face was made up with ten tonnes of make-up. She didn't care if others loved that, but it was a choice and hers had been made for her enough over the last decade. She was finally finding out who she was and if she died out here in the freezing cold, she'd never get to see the beauty of the life she could have with Bram.

Fighting the sleepy feeling, Aoife looked around for some way to break the ropes on her hands but all she saw was rock. Knowing she had no other choice, she shrugged the blanket off her shoulders and leaned into the rock, trying to find a sharp corner to rub the rope against.

Pain made her whimper as the hard unforgiving stone cut not only the rope but her skin. Blood, warm and wet, oozed over her hands making her fingers slip as she tried to grip the rope to give her more leverage. She was almost through when she heard footsteps outside the cave. Desperation made her saw her arms faster against the hard surface as pain made her almost blind with agony.

"No, no. What are you doing?"

Aoife cried out as Boyd grabbed her upper arm pulling her away from the rock and shoving her to her side. For a second, hopelessness weighed so heavy she could only lie there and cry. He yanked the gag from her mouth and looked at her with triumph. She knew then the money was in the account as he'd asked and that her father would be coming for her soon.

"You stupid woman, look what you've done to yourself."

Aoife felt her tears dry as anger took over as she struggled to sit up. "Me? What *I've* done? You did this. You hogtied me, kidnapped me, and from the look on your ugly face, you told him where I am."

"He'll be here in six hours, or as soon as they can get the flight moving."

"Congratulations, you just killed me. Hope it was worth it."

"You'll never understand."

Aoife snorted. "What? How you want to avenge your rapist brother?"

"Don't say that," Boyd screamed, his face going red as he pulled her from the place she sat and shoved her to the ground. His boot hit her hard when it landed in her belly, the next in her ribs making her lose her breath. But she wouldn't give him the satisfaction of begging.

"You're nothing but a murderer and your brother is a rapist scum bag. I hope Bram finds you and kills you just like he did the little weasel you called a brother."

As blow after blow fell, unconsciousness pricked at her, and she welcomed the comfort of the darkness. There was no cold or pain here, just blissful peace. Bram would come, she knew he would. She had to believe he'd come because she had nothing else left to give.

CHAPTER 27

When he set foot on his home soil, Bram was met by Rory and three other experienced trackers he knew for a fact could track as well as he could. One was his old teacher, Ian, another the man who'd taken him through his Gold Duke of Edinburgh award.

"Thank you for coming. I can't tell you how much this means to me."

"Rory explained that lunatic Boyd Walsh has kidnapped your girl. What do you need from us?"

Bás was dealing with the imminent threat from Doyle and setting up comms and a defensive position from the castle, as well as seeing if they could go offensive before they got there. That left him and Rory free to find Aoife with the help of his old friends. Snow had wanted to help him but he knew she'd be more use giving Bás the tour of the castle and grounds.

Bram laid a map out on the bonnet of the Range Rover and circled the three positions he knew were the most likely routes Boyd would've used. "Ian, you and Graham take this route that heads over the bluff to the river. Jock, can you and Winnie head towards the bridge that meets up with the village and make sure he hasn't gone through there?" Bram glanced at the golden retriever who was sitting loyally at her master's feet waiting for instructions. "I can give you a scarf that belongs to Aoife to see if Winnie picks up the scent."

"Aye, that we can."

Bram glanced at Rory who looked like he'd aged by ten years since that morning and Bram wondered if he looked the same way and felt he probably did. "You and I'll head toward the caves on the east side."

"That area has a sheer drop on the other side."

"Yeah, I know and that's why it's perfect. He won't have to watch his back so much, and the caves will give him shelter from the elements. Don't forget he wants Aoife alive so he needs a place to hunker down."

"Fair point."

"We all have our radios. Only use them in an emergency or if you find something significant. Stay safe and please don't put yourself in danger. If you find them radio in. Do not approach Boyd. He has a gun and is a desperate man by the sounds of it, but he's also a very cunning one."

The others nodded and headed out, slipping into the woods silently like the hunters they were. He and Rory headed toward the lawn and the direction he felt in his gut Boyd had taken Aoife. Since the second he'd arrived and had seen the scene in the bedroom and walked the tunnels, he'd felt his calm descend as if the detachment he needed to find her and do his job had pulled him from the man in love to a man hell-bent on bringing her home.

They walked in silence. Rory was concerned as he was with the added weight of guilt he didn't need to be carrying. He hadn't been able to look Bram in the eye since he'd arrived, and he understood the feeling. It had taken him months to be able to look at Lana without the feeling of shame almost crushing him.

They stopped a few times as he checked a broken branch or touched his fingers to a partial footprint. Every step he took he was more certain this was the way they'd come. Even though Boyd had done a decent job of hiding his tracks, Bram was better.

"I know that feeling of guilt, Rory, and in this instance it's misplaced."

"I should've checked on them, made sure I knew exactly who was in our home."

"We all make mistakes, and you couldn't have foreseen that a man hell-bent on revenge for something I did over a decade ago was a threat. This is on me not you."

"It's my family, I should've done better."

"I know that feeling, Rory. God knows I've been feeling it nearly all my life."

"Lana doesn't blame you, you know." Rory glanced across at him, his ruddy face craggy with worry.

"And neither do I. You need to forgive yourself for what happened to Lana. She never blamed you, and it hurts her to know you still carry this. Let me tell you from experience if you really want to love Aoife like she deserves and be the man she needs, then you need to forgive yourself for being human."

Bram huffed out a humourless laugh. "I wish it was that simple, but I don't think I can do that. The fact will always remain that if I'd let her stay in that pub it wouldn't have happened."

"Of course it would. Ray was obsessed with Lana and he would've found a way to do what he did. It wouldn't have stopped anything, just postponed it and maybe you wouldn't have been there to make sure she got the justice she deserved."

Bram knew that Rory was aware of what he'd done to Ray Walsh, Lana had admitted it to him a long time ago.

"For the record, I wish I could've done the same thing. If I could drag him from the ground and do the same thing I would have. Fuck forgiveness. That man didn't deserve to breathe air, and I'm glad you killed him."

"It was unintentional, I can assure you. I just saw red and deep down I do regret that I took him from his family, but not that I stopped him from having the freedom to do it again. Also, for the shame I know I brought my own parents and the pain I caused them. I was meant to be the perfect son, instead, I was nothing but a disappointment to them both. You were the son they should've had, Rory, and I'm glad my sister has you."

Rory stopped and Bram turned to him, a look of pensiveness on his face. "Bram, you need to read your father's letter."

Bram went to respond to his brother-in-law's words when a sliver of light caught on something shiny, and he bent to the fallen, rotting leaves and saw the tiny silver four-leaf clover. His heart began to race as he pulled the bracelet that he'd placed on Aoife's wrist not two weeks ago.

She'd seen it in the window of a shop in the town over and fallen in love. Snow had gone in and bought it for him, and he'd given it to her later that night before they'd made love by the fire in his room.

Rory moved closer. "What is it?"

"It's the bracelet I bought Aoife." Bram smiled. "Which means we're on the right track. I know she was wearing it this morning when I left."

"Let's move then."

Bram didn't need to be asked twice as they picked up their speed, not needing to move at such a painstakingly slow rate to watch for clues. He'd hold off on radioing the others until he was sure though. He knew in this cold Aoife was at serious risk of exposure, apart from whatever else that bastard may have done to her. If Boyd had laid this as a trap, he didn't want to call the others off and halve their chances of finding her. In his gut though, he knew they were on the right track; he could feel her close.

They were around three hundred metres from the caves where he suspected Boyd would take Aoife when he heard the scream. The hair on the back of his neck stood on end as he glanced at Rory, who'd had the same reaction if the look on his face was any indication.

The two men drew their weapons and took off in the direction of the sound, Bram's heart beating out of his chest in his race to get to Aoife before Boyd could hurt her. Reaching the caves, he quickly followed the directions of the shouting and screaming and stopped for a split second, his whole world flipping on its head as he saw Aoife on the dirty, wet floor covered in blood as Boyd drew his leg back to kick her.

As if transported back in time, it was like watching Ray Walsh again, and the rage he felt in his blood was boiling over. Without conscious thought, he grabbed Boyd, dragging him off Aoife and hauling him to the entrance to the cave before throwing him to the ground. Through vision almost red with fury, he launched himself at the man, his fist hitting his cheekbone, the crack not even registering as Boyd fell screaming to the ground. Not satisfied, Bram straddled the man, laying punch after punch as Boyd tried to fight back with no chance against a man more trained than he'd ever be, and one full of rage.

"Bram, no. Stop. Please."

The light touch on his shoulder brought him out of the inhuman anger and he fell back, Boyd forgotten as he stumbled toward Aoife and took her in his arms. He kissed her gently, running his hands all over her as he looked for injuries.

"You're bleeding. He hurt you."

"I tried to escape and cut my arms on the rocks."

"He kicked you." He held her now like she was porcelain as he shed his jacket and wrapped her in the thermal blanket Rory handed him.

"It's over now and I've had worse."

Bram clenched his teeth, his brain barely handling this attack on her without thinking what else she'd been subjected to over the years. "I'm so sorry I let this happen."

"What? No, this isn't on you. Boyd is lost and needs help, but Bram, he told my father where we are."

"I know. My team is back at the castle making preparations."

"Okay, good."

"I found this." Bram held the bracelet up for her to see and she smiled so wide it lit up the sky and burned off the cold.

"I hoped you'd find it."

"It was clever. We might make a tracker out of you yet."

Aoife laughed but it ended with a whimper, and he knew she was in more pain than she was letting on.

"Let's get you home and get the doctor to take a look at you."

"Bram, wait. Is Lana, okay?"

Bram looked at Rory, who was watching the snivelling Boyd, with a rifle aimed at his head. "She will be."

"Good, and Mrs Murrel?"

"Is tough, and apparently awake but she'll be in the hospital for a while recovering."

"That makes me madder than anything. That he dragged Mrs M into this and hurt her. She was innocent."

"You're innocent, Aoife."

"Maybe."

Bram didn't like the way she said that, but he didn't want to get into it now with Boyd listening and Aoife cold and injured. He radioed Bás and asked for an ATV to be brought as close as they could get it and to send someone to pick up Boyd. They didn't have time to hang around when the chances were that Doyle was on his way and the next battle was about to commence.

CHAPTER 28

"B RAM, I CAN WALK. YOU DON'T NEED TO CARRY ME." AOIFE PROTESTED BUT the truth was she enjoyed being in his arms, a feeling of safety which she clung to, knowing how quickly it could be taken from her.

"Hush, I like carrying you."

Aoife smiled but winced as he set her down in front of the roaring fire in the main living room used by the family when they were at the castle. Warmth instantly began to seep into her veins, the cold loosening its painful hold on her body.

Snow rushed in and came toward Aoife, dropping to her knees at her feet and wrapping her arms gently around her in a show of affection she hadn't expected. She and Snow had grown close but neither one was a naturally tactile person unless they were close. Yet she leaned into her new friends embrace.

"You scared the heck out of me."

"I'm sorry, Snow."

Snow looked her over in a similar way that Bram had done.

"I'm going to get the first aid kit. Can you stay with her, Snow?"

Bram was already on his feet, knowing his teammate would stay. Aoife wanted to protest that she didn't need a babysitter, but she knew this was for his peace of mind and for him she'd do almost anything.

"Did he hurt you?"

"A few kicks here and there, nothing that won't heal."

"I've never seen Bram so shaken. When he heard you were gone, I thought he was going to lose his mind with worry."

"I hate that he went through that, but it's over for now."

"Hmm."

Bram came back in the room with a first aid box, Bás and Lotus following behind with a man she hadn't met.

"Glad to have you back, Aoife."

"I'm sorry for causing this mess."

Bás sat on the opposite couch as Bram began to tend to her damaged wrists, the sting of the antiseptic making her breath hiss.

"Nonsense, this is nobody's fault but the man who did it, and now he's being taken into custody to answer for his crimes."

"He needs help, he's sick."

"Perhaps, but that's for the courts to decide. We have more pressing issues. Doyle has left London on a flight that didn't file a manifest, so we can't track it, but I think it's safe to assume he's coming here."

Aoife shivered, partly from cold but mostly from the thought of her father's imminent arrival. She'd never become immune to the fear he could incite in her. He was the man who'd taught her to ride a bike when she was six, and then beat her the following day for skinning her knee and marring her skin. He gave affection out like scraps of meat and for so many years she yearned for his love until she learned he didn't know how to love anyone. Now it was merely fear and hatred she felt for him. "What will we do?"

"My people are setting up at strategic points around the castle, but I could do with Bram's help."

"Two minutes and this will be done." Bram's voice was firm, but his touch gentle as he finished wrapping her wrists in gauze.

She touched his forearm, feeling his strength as the muscle

rippled beneath her fingers. "You should go, nobody knows this castle better than you."

"I will as soon as I'm sure you're okay."

The worry for her was mixed in with what she knew was his guilt and she hated that he felt that way and needed him to understand. Turning she looked at Bás as she saw Lotus and the mystery man talking in hushed whispers as they left the room.

"Can you give us a minute, please?"

Bás watched her for just a second before he nodded and stood, clearing the room, and leaving just her and Bram.

"Bram, do you blame me for this mess I've dragged your team into?"

His frown deepened across his brow. "No of course not, this isn't your fault. Doyle is sick and evil, and his failings are his own. Why would you ask me that?" He paced in front of the fire, running his hands in through his hair, but still not looking at her.

"Bram, please come sit down a second."

Bram stopped and came to sit beside her, his thigh warm against her own in the warm, dry fleece pants she now wore thanks to Snow. Angling her body toward him she took his hand in her own and laid it against her cheek, watching his features soften with his feeling for her.

"Boyd wasn't your fault, Bram, just like my father isn't mine. It was a horrible set of circumstances, but it wasn't your fault."

"I killed his brother in cold blood. I beat him to death with my bare hands and got away with it."

She knew he was trying to shock her, to push her away and it wouldn't work. "Why?"

"Because he raped Lana."

"Oh, Bram, do you really think I'd love you any less for defending your sister from the man who raped her? That I don't know what it is to want someone evil dead? You didn't kill because you suddenly decided it was a fun idea, you protected your family and I love you for it. I love all of you."

His eyes lit up with love and desire she knew was never far from the surface when they were together. "I love you too, Irish. I don't know what I did to deserve a precious jewel like you, but I know I don't deserve you."

"You do, Bram. We both deserve to be happy."

Bram's lips found her own in a sweet tender kiss that had her body heating in a way the fire never could. His hands caressed her scalp, holding her still for his kiss until she sighed against him as he pulled away. "I love you, Bram. Now go help your team figure out how to end this so we can look forward not back."

Taking her hand, he pulled her to her feet. "We do this together as a team."

Aoife grinned as she followed him out of the room and towards the noise and commotion in what she knew was his father's old office. Bás looked across at them holding hands and winked at her, making her blush and Bram growled, making Titan laugh.

"Okay, now the love birds have their shit worked out, can we make a plan, please? It's way too fucking cold up here for me."

Bram stepped in front of the desk and began to layout the best positions around the castle. "We don't have as much firepower as I'd like, but we have the tactical and skill advantage. As we know from the men Doyle sent before, they aren't highly trained, rather they're paid muscle. We have eyes in the village that will give us warning when they hit the area so nobody can sneak up on us and we have a good defensive position. If we use the tunnels inside the walls, we can corral them into this area here and take them out."

Lotus crossed her arms as she looked at the map. "You want me to go high?"

Bram pointed to a tower on the west side near the gatehouse. "If you position yourself here with Hurricane on the ground with Titan, we can get in behind them. Bás and Snow, if you loop in here, we can herd them towards the central point. Myself, Rykov, and Aoife will be in the walls here and block off any escape. Watchdog, you have full overview. Doyle doesn't walk out of here." Bram looked at her then Bás, who nodded and took over.

"That's a solid plan. As for the others, take them alive if you can but don't put yourself at risk to do so. Remember, these men are evil, and we have a green light from the higher-ups to take this down." Bás glanced at Rykov. "Are your men ready to go in Dublin as soon as we pull the cord?"

"Yes, everything is in position, and they're awaiting my word."

"And Popov is under control?"

"My men have that situation handled."

Aoife was confused as to who the mystery man was but suspected he might be the Russian Bratva contact Lotus had discussed.

"So, we're all set?"

Bram looked down at his phone and she felt him brace. "Good, because they're here."

"Everyone, take your positions and keep the comms open. Watchdog, you have control."

Aoife took the gun Snow and Bram had taught her how to shoot and followed the man she loved up the stairs, with the man called Rykov behind them so they could slip into the walls of the castle where wars and battles had been won and lost for generations. It was time to end this.

CHAPTER 29

THE SILENCE WAS DEAFENING AS SHE WAITED BESIDE BRAM FOR THE FIGHT TO begin. Her belly in knots, her hands shaking, not with fear but with anticipation of this being over, whatever the outcome and she prayed fearlessly that it would be in their favour. She believed for the first time in years that it would be, but whatever happened she knew this was her last stand. She had no more running in her and she had no desire to run either.

She'd stand and fight beside this man she loved and who by some miracle loved her, and if she went down then so be it.

"Target is in sight."

"Let them through, Lotus. I want eyes on Doyle."

Aoife had never worn a comms in her ear before and the sound of a voice made her jump. The feel of Bram's hand on her back steadied her nerves.

"I have Doyle in sight. He's in a vehicle behind the lead car."

She thought that was Hurricane she heard but the comm unit made it difficult to tell between him and Watchdog, as they both had deep baritones.

Bram looked down at a small handheld device and she could see the four cars roll into view exactly where Bram wanted them. The lights on the castle had all been extinguished so it looked abandoned, which was what they wanted Doyle to think so he'd relax his guard and get out of the car.

Looking over his shoulder she saw shadowed movement as men got out of the back two cars and began to walk toward the castle, heavy semi-automatic weapons hanging from their hands.

"*Bás, Snow, are you in position?*"

"*Yes.*"

"*Lotus, Hurricane, Titan, take out the tires on the cars.*"

Aoife tensed as the pops from the gunshots took out the tires and her father's men began to fire. Shadow returned fire, taking out her father's guards with little fuss. Suddenly an explosion rocked the foundations under her feet and her hands braced against Bram.

"*What the fuck? Sitrep, now.*"

"*Explosion on the north side of the castle.*"

Aoife felt anguish roil in her belly at the thought of the beautiful ballroom being damaged.

Bram gestured to Rykov to head back up toward the bedroom. "We need to get out of the tunnels in case the explosion has done structural damage."

Back in the bedroom, Bram checked the screen on his device. "*We got eyes on Doyle?*"

"*Negative. We lost sight of him when the explosion blew.*"

"*Fuck, someone find him.*"

Aoife could hear Watchdog directing people in certain directions with Bás interjecting instructions.

"*Snow's been hit.*"

Bás words were like ice-cold water being thrown over her body.

"*Get her to the library and we'll meet you there.*"

More gunfire filled the comms unit as the three of them moved down the stairs. A man rounded the corner and Bram took him out with a single headshot. As they descended the stairs two more attacked from the side. Aoife was thrown sideways, her head hitting off the dado rail at the bottom of the stairs. Rykov was fighting two men hand to hand as Bram held off a swathe that came through the door.

"I need help in the main front hall."

Aoife remembered the gun in her hand and fired at a man about to shoot Rykov in the back. He fell, holding his side and Rykov turned with a grin so sexy she thought it would melt the fires of hell.

"Thanks."

"Aoife, get to the library and help Snow. I need Bás with me."

It was only a few feet, but it felt like miles as the bullets flew and the grunts of people fighting filled her ears. Moving toward the library, her back against the wall, she felt like a coward running away when they were fighting men that seemed to multiply as fast as they fell.

Pushing down on the door handle, she knew her leaving was for the best and Bás would be way more help than she ever would.

Closing the door, she looked around in the darkness and wished she had a light to help her. With no streetlights, the only light they had was on the weapons and the night vision goggles the others wore. She now wished she'd accepted them when offered but she found them too confusing and disorientating.

"Aoife?"

"Snow?" Aoife rushed toward the sound and found Snow leaning against the back of the couch. She couldn't see much more but could hear the pain in her voice.

"Where are you hurt?"

"Caught a damn bullet in my side. Don't think it's life threatening but I can't run. Bás totally overreacted and sent me in here."

"What can I do?"

"Watch the door. I need to watch the window."

"I can do that."

The sounds of gunfire were getting less now, and she could hear the tides turning in their favour. But her father was still missing, that slippery son of a bitch had probably escaped again.

Just as the thought entered her head, a sound from the opposite side of the room made the hair on the back of her neck stand on end.

"Oh, Aoife. Is that my princess I hear?"

Snow gripped her hand tight, and she wished again she could see in the darkness. It wasn't as bad as before, her eyes slowly adjusting but all she could make out was shadows and the voice which could paralyse her with fear.

"Now, don't hide from me. I just want you to come home where you belong."

Aoife turned her body toward the direction she could hear him and saw his outline in the dying embers of the fire that had been extinguished in haste.

Aoife moved sideways so she could keep him in sight, knowing that her heart was probably beating loud enough to give her position away.

"It's over, Aoife. You need to do your duty and come home. I've had enough of this shite from you."

Anger was building inside her as she moved closer so she could face him. Standing, she raised her gun and her father swung around to face her.

"There she is, my little princess."

"I'm not your anything. You're nothing to me but my jailer and captor." She could see he had a weapon trained on her too and if she had to die taking this evil man from the world then so be it but first, she'd tell him what she really thought. "You're a coward, a murderer, and a sexual predator. You don't care about anyone but yourself."

"You ungrateful bitch. You're the biggest disappointment of my life. I should've strangled you at birth."

"No wonder my mother hated you."

"She was nothing but a whore anyway."

"I hope you rot in hell."

Doyle stepped forward, his voice a snarl. "I'll rule hell like I rule here. Nobody can stop me. I have so much power that even behind bars I'll find you, not that I'll be there long. I have friends in very high places. I'll take pleasure in making sure you and all your little friends are tortured and kept alive for years to come so you can suffer."

"Oh, you mistook me, I didn't mean prison I meant actual hell."

As Doyle laughed Aoife fired, squeezing the trigger like Bram had taught her, the sound exploding in her head as she heard it hit the wall behind her father. His laughter filled her ears and she realised she'd failed again, and he wouldn't give her another chance to try and kill him. As he raised his gun, she went to dive behind the couch, but another bullet sounded, and she watched as Doyle stilled for a second before his body fell forward, revealing the silhouette of the man she loved behind him.

Bram stepped closer to her father's fallen body and fired twice more as she looked on with so many emotions going through her body and mind it was all she could do to stay standing. Relief, disbelief, fear, anger, grief, and love for the man who'd set her free.

Bram rushed towards her and took her in his arms, holding her tight to his body as he whispered words of comfort and love which she could hardly comprehend as she wept, all the stress of the last few days suddenly sucking every last drop of energy from her body.

As the gunfire stopped and the threat was finally over, she looked down at the man who'd given her life, only to steal every ounce of joy from it over and over again and struggled to believe it was over.

The lights came on and Bás and Titan rushed in, moving to Snow who was watching her with a smile through her pain.

"You did good, Aoife. Your shot was shit, but you moved him into a position where Bram could take him and kept him talking."

Aoife crouched beside her friend and held her hand as they moved her to the couch so she could be patched up and flown to the closest hospital.

"I'd like to say it was intentional, but it was all emotional instinct."

An arm came around her and Bram kissed her head. "Bullshit, you're a natural. What do you say Bás, you reckon we have room in the team for her?"

Bás raised an eyebrow and Aoife laughed.

"Actually, I think I want to give nursing a go."

Titan pointed at her. "Now, that we definitely need on this team."

As her father lay lifeless on the floor, she had to thank him in some ways because without him, she may never have met the man she loved or the people she knew would be her family until her dying day.

CHAPTER 30

Leaning back, Bram took a swig of the whisky his father had loved so much, feeling the heat of it slide smoothly down his throat. For forty minutes he'd sat in his father's chair at his desk, looking at the envelope that was now fraying at the edges from wear.

Aoife was sleeping upstairs after the clean-up from the battle with Doyle and his death. It had been like a plug had been pulled and every ounce of energy had left her. He knew it would take months, perhaps years before she truly relaxed in the knowledge that her nightmare was over. He also knew it would be a lot longer before he forgave himself for his part in her kidnapping.

Turning the envelope over again, he listened to the sounds of the castle settling into sleep. The team had stayed overnight and would head back to Hereford tomorrow. Rykov had gone to Ireland to make sure the takeover had gone as smoothly as such a thing could.

He knew he'd put it off long enough and tore open the letter from his father, the familiar script causing an ache in his chest that he hadn't expected or prepared for. He'd always been closer to his father, his mother's injury causing her to withdraw, and he knew with the gift of hindsight that it had been his dad that had tried to keep the family together.

Forcing his eyes to the words he read.

Dear Bram,

If you're reading this, then I'm no longer of this world. It may be self-ish, but I pray that I go with your mother. I don't know if I could survive this place without her love. Our story is one that I should've told you sooner but there never seemed like a good time, and while I don't regret loving her and having the life I had, I do regret the pain I caused.

When I was twenty, I was promised to a woman I didn't love. Rosalie Walsh was young and beautiful, and we knew each other well, but we weren't in love, at least I wasn't in love. I didn't know at the time, but she was in love with me. I blame myself for not seeing the truth.

An arrangement was made for us to marry, but I wanted one last summer of freedom first and it was agreed. While I was away, I met your mother. She was the most stunning creature I'd ever laid eyes on. We fell in love. I told her of my promise to another and not once did she try and force me into something I couldn't give her. She simply showed me love and fun and by the end of the summer, I knew I couldn't leave her.

I don't know if you'll ever understand a love like that, but I pray you do. She was my heart and soul, so we married in secret, and I brought her home. Your grandfather was furious, but the marriage promise to Rosalie was already broken. I thought over time people would get over it.

I never dreamed for a second Rosalie would kill herself, that to her the marriage and engagement was real. I'll never forgive myself for her pain and I know your mother always held misplaced guilt over her death too.

That's the reason for the rift between our families, but I never believed it would spill over into the lives of my children.

The night I got the call about Ray Walsh attacking your sister is the worst of my life. I've never been so furious or felt so impotent. To have your child go through what she did is something I hope you never experience. Yet, that same night left me with a pride I'll never forget.

In you, my son. You defended your sister in a way I never did, you sought out the criminal and handed out retribution. You did what I couldn't. I'm so proud to call you my son, to know that you'll stand up for the weak and won't be afraid to do what's needed. My only regret for you was that it would cost you your future. That's why I called Jack Granger. He was a student when I taught a class as a guest lecturer at the camp and became a friend despite the age difference and through our connections with the royal family we became closer, I'd heard word he may be able to help. I never dreamed he could make it all go away the way it did, but I'm proud of how you took the chance and made something of your life.

I'll always be sorry that I never said this in person, but I'm not sure I could have.

Be happy, my son, know that my pride in you and my love for you are infinite.

Love always,

Dad

BRAM SAT BACK IN SHOCK, the page falling from his grasp as the enormity of the revelations hit him. The secrets his father and mother had kept, the pride and love his father had for him. For years he'd thought he was the black sheep, the disappointment, and yet it was his father who'd sent him salvation.

His father who'd given him the life he hadn't known he wanted or needed, and he was proud of the man he was, despite his knowledge of what he'd done. To kill was one thing but to kill with your bare fists was raw and brutal, yet he didn't see him like that. He'd thought he was a good son, a fine man.

Was he right? Was there good in him, a man worthy of the love of a woman like Aoife? For the first time in his life, he was beginning to think maybe he was worthy.

Folding the letter and placing it back in the envelope, Bram tucked it in his jacket and left the study, switching off the light as he went.

At the door to his bedroom, he stood in the light and watched the woman he loved sleep, her body in the middle of the huge bed curled into a ball. Bram shed his clothes and climbed in beside her, hauling her body into his arms and holding her as she snuggled back against him.

"You okay?"

Her hand rubbed his arm in a comforting gesture, her voice barely a whisper in the darkness. "I am now."

"I love you, Bram."

"I love you too, Aoife. You're the only thing that matters to me. Not my job, not this place, nothing."

He kissed her shoulder, only pulling back as she rolled to look at him. "What do you mean by that?"

"If you want me to walk away from Shadow to be with you, I'll do it. If you want to be a lady of the manor then we'll do that with Lana and Rory. Whatever you need to be happy I'll do, Aoife, because you're all that matters to me."

Her fingers traced the seam of his lips, and he nipped the pads of her fingers.

"I want to have a normal life. I want to go back to school to work and get my nursing degree, which I can do in Hereford. Birmingham University is close and Worcester even closer. You could continue working for Shadow and we can live in the village. I know you don't think it but what you do is necessary, and you're good at it. Shadow needs you and I think we need them too."

Bram felt his heart race. Was he really getting everything he wanted handed to him on a plate? "Are you sure?"

"Yes. Snow and Titan have become friends and I love the village life where we have people who care about us."

"I guess Shadow is part of my family. We may be slightly dysfunctional but when I needed them, they didn't hesitate."

Bram knew there'd be lots more to figure out, but for now, he knew where they were going and that they'd do it together—them against the world.

EPILOGUE

"Where are we going, Bram?"

Her man had a hold of her hand as he led her blindfolded out of their home into the warm spring sunshine. "I told you it's a surprise."

Aoife shook her head in mock irritation, but the truth was she trusted him and if he said she'd like it she knew she would. The last six months had been blissful, and she kept waiting for the bubble to burst, for her life to fall back into the pattern of destruction it was before she'd found this place and these people.

They were now living in a two-bedroom house in the village, although Bram kept his quarters at the facility, which they'd use sometimes too if things were on high alert or they just wanted to spend some time with their friends there. She was back working at the pub and Bram was doing his thing with Shadow.

She had everything she'd never known she missed. A man who adored her, friends like Snow, Lotus, and Duchess and surrogate brothers in the shape of the Shadow Elite men. In the autumn, she'd start her nursing degree and have almost everything she'd ever dreamed of.

The rest would come in time. Marriage and kids were all on the agenda for the future and something she and Bram talked about in the wee hours when it was just the two of them. Her life, the one she'd run from, was like a bad dream and, with the help of a counsellor, she was learning to accept the things she'd been through and deal with them.

Feeling the air on her cheeks, she tilted her head up to feel the waning sun on her face. She'd never grow weary of this place. It soothed her soul in a way no other place except perhaps the castle did.

"Watch your step."

Aoife lifted her leg, trying not to feel like an idiot as she felt for the step up. The second she felt the warmth and smelled the familiar comforting scent of hops, she knew where she was.

"Did you bring me to the pub where I spend every night as my surprise?" Aoife didn't mind but she was confused.

Firm lips took hers in a kiss that made her toes curl and, despite not being able to see, she leaned in, wrapping her arms around his neck. This was something else she'd never get tired of, this man and the way he could kiss her until the world disappeared.

Pulling away he touched his fingers to the blindfold. "Happy birthday, Irish."

As the blindfold fell away, the room erupted with a chorus of singing as all her friends began to sing. Peyton, Snow, Titan, Hurricane, Reaper, Duchess, Bishop, Watchdog, Bás—they were all there smiling at her from the bar.

Her eyes fell on Lana and Rory, who was holding three-month-old Danny in his arms, the other children right beside them grinning at her, and in the corner was Mrs Murrel with a huge smile on her face.

"How?"

Bram was looking at her with so much love it was hard to breathe. "Peyton told me."

Aoife had wanted to keep her birthday a low-key secret and had been holding off on telling Bram when it was. Years of disappointment had shown her that birthdays were not to be celebrated so she'd stopped.

"You might not want to celebrate the day you were born but to me, it was the greatest day of my life, I just didn't know it at the time."

"Bram?"

Tears hit her eyes at his beautiful words and the sentiment behind them. She thought he'd hug her, but he stepped away and as the space behind him cleared, he dropped to one knee making her gasp as the realisation caught up with her.

Through bleary eyes, Aoife watched as Bram produced a small ring box and flicked the lid to show an antique diamond ring she knew had been his mother's. Knowing the story behind their love made this all the more special.

"Aoife, from the second I set foot in this bar, and you blew me off with your sweet rebuff, I was captivated. I think I knew then that you were about to change my life forever. We've been through some challenges, some painful, others exciting. Through it all watching you become the person you are today and loving every single transition in between, I've been hooked. Your sweetness, your kindness, your ability to befriend just about anyone, but most of all your strength and resilience."

She was shaking now, his words hitting her so hard.

"I'll never know what I did to make me deserve you, but I do know that I'll spend every day of my life making you happy. Will you marry me?"

Aoife didn't wait, she hurled herself into his arms knowing he'd catch her, his lips meeting her own as tears mingled with the sweetness of his kiss. Bram thought he was the lucky one, but she knew the truth—she was the one who was lucky to have this man love her and want her forever and she'd happily give it.

"Yes, yes, a hundred times yes."

As cheers went up around the room, Bram held her tight and she knew he'd never let go because he was hers and she was his and she'd change nothing about her past if it led her to this beautiful life. No, Aoife would guard her salvation with her life, and she knew he'd do the same.

SNEAK PEEK: INNOCENT SALVATION

"Snow, what can I do for you?"

Snow placed the printout she'd been looking at for the last two hours on Bás' desk.

He picked it up and read the names on the list before his head raised to look at her. "What is this?"

"Watchdog found it in Doyle's files."

Bás leaned back in his chair regarding her as she tried not to fidget and show how much she had invested in this. "And?"

"You know who those people are?"

Bás snorted and picked up the paper again. "Dominique Dupont and Sebastian Alexander." He looked at her again and motioned for her to sit, which she did. "Tell me what's going on with you, Snow, and don't fucking lie to me."

Snow considered lying. She needed this job and Bás would go ballistic if he found out she was keeping secrets. It was the one thing he wouldn't tolerate. "I want to know what Dominique and Judge Alexander are involved with."

Bás showed no emotion at all when she said the woman's name

and she wondered if he already knew her background and guessed it was a possibility. "Why now? What caused this sudden interest?"

Snow produced a picture of a little girl no more than six years old, her sweet face smiling at the camera. Her heart clenched with pain, and she had to hold a hand to her belly to steady herself. Pushing the image toward Bás, she swallowed the bile in her throat. "Because that's my niece that Judge Alexander is raising, and I want to know why."

Snow thought Bás would react but still nothing, and it was frustrating.

"How is this Shadow business?"

Snow clenched her fist and released it hoping she could remain calm. Her personality was bright and cheery, but she had a quick temper that got her into trouble. "Judge Alexander is leading the inquiry into the corruption trial against the men who helped Doyle. If he's dirty, then it's our business."

"Is it just Alexander you're interested in or Dominique too?"

Just her name made Snow see red. The woman swanned around like she shit roses, making speeches and acting as if she were the epitome of perfection and truth, and yet she was the dirtiest of them all. "She's as dirty as hell, and you know it as well as I do."

"I do know that but going after her isn't something we'd do lightly. A woman like her will have her skeletons well hidden. She won't take risks with her reputation, and you can bet your ass she has people to deal with these things for her."

"Oh, I know that better than most but there's one skeleton she can't walk away from and I can prove it."

"Oh?"

"She murdered my father."

Bás raised his one brow for her to keep going. "How do you know this?"

"Because I watched her do it when I was sixteen years old." Snow waved her hand in the air. "She didn't actually fire the gun, but she stood and watched as her men tortured and killed him."

"Why would she want him dead?"

"Because he held the key to her weakness."

"And that is?"

"Me! I'm the key because I'm the daughter she gave away like rubbish and told my father to dispose of. I'm the daughter of the President of France and it's time she paid for her crimes." She was breathing hard, the pain of reliving the worst day of her life taking its toll on her nerves.

"I take it if you're here you have a plan?"

Snow tried not to show her excitement but failed as she leaned forward. "Alexander needs a nanny for the girl. I can get in and find the proof we need of any involvement or corruption and check on my niece at the same time."

"You really think getting up close and personal is a good idea? Duchess and Lotus normally handle the undercover work?"

"No, this is mine. I can do this, Bás."

"Judge Alexander won't be a pushover. He's the youngest court of appeals judge in history at thirty-five and has the money behind him to back up his power. He's old money and has a reputation as a hardass. You sure you can handle that? He's the antithesis to your sunny disposition."

"I'm there for the kid. You just need to make sure I get an interview and I can do the rest."

"Fine, but you don't go alone. I want Reaper to go with you. Use the flat in Kensington and pretend he's your roommate."

"Fine."

"I'll call a meeting and inform the others of the plan." Bás linked his fingers and leaned forward. "But if I think for one second you've lost control or gone off-book, I'll pull you out faster than you can blink."

"I won't let you down, Bás."

"It's not me I'm worried about."

Snow walked from the room and headed back to her quarters. Going to her desk she took out the image of Sebastian Alexander. He

217

was a handsome devil. He had dark hair with a slight curl that was barely contained, tanned skin, a strong jaw, and he filled a suit in a way that male models would hang themselves from the rafters for.

It didn't matter though, because she'd never be attracted to a man who could smile at Dominique like he was in this picture. No, a man like that would never have her heart or her body. He was the enemy, and she was going to destroy him.

http://mybook.to/Innocentsalvation

218

WANT A FREE SHORT STORY?

Sign up for Maddie's Newsletter using the link below and receive a free copy of the short story, Fortis: Where it all Began.

When hard-nosed SAS operator, Zack Cunningham is forced to work a mission with the fiery daughter of the American General, sparks fly. As those heated looks turn into scorching hot stolen kisses, a forbidden love affair begins that neither had expected.

Just as life is looking perfect disaster strikes and Ava Drake is left wondering if she will ever see the man she loves again.

https://dl.bookfunnel.com/cyrjtv3tta

BOOKS BY MADDIE WADE

FORTIS SECURITY

Healing Danger (Dane and Lauren)

Stolen Dreams (Nate and Skye)

Love Divided (Jace and Lucy)

Secret Redemption (Zack and Ava)

Broken Butterfly (Zin and Celeste)

Arctic Fire (Kanan and Roz)

Phoenix Rising (Daniel and Megan)

Nate & Skye Wedding Novella

Digital Desire (Will and Aubrey)

Paradise Ties: A Fortis Wedding Novella (Jace and Lucy & Dane and Lauren)

Wounded Hearts (Drew and Mara)

Scarred Sunrise (Smithy and Lizzie)

Zin and Celeste: A Fortis Family Christmas

Fortis Boxset 1 (Books 1-3)

Fortis Boxset 2 (Books 4-7.5

EIDOLON

Alex

Blake

Reid

Liam

Mitch

Gunner

Waggs

Jack

Lopez

Decker

ALLIANCE AGENCY SERIES (CO-WRITTEN WITH INDIA KELLS)

Deadly Alliance

Knight Watch

Hidden Obsession

Lethal Justice

Innocent Target

Power Play

RYOSHI DELTA (PART OF SUSAN STOKER'S POLICE AND FIRE: OPERATION ALPHA WORLD)

Condor's Vow

Sandstorm's Promise

Hawk's Honor

Omega's Oath

SHADOW ELITE

Guarding Salvation

Innocent Salvation

TIGHTROPE DUET

Tightrope One

Tightrope Two

ANGELS OF THE TRIAD

01 Sariel

OTHER WORLDS

Keeping Her Secrets *Suspenseful Seduction World* (Samantha A. Cole's World)

Finding English P*olice and Fire: Operation Alpha* (Susan Stoker's world)

About the Author

Contact Me

If stalking an author is your thing and I sure hope it is then here are the links to my social media pages.

If you prefer your stalking to be more intimate, then my group Maddie's Minxes will welcome you with open arms.

General Email: info.maddiewade@gmail.com
Email: maddie@maddiewadeauthor.co.uk
Website: http://www.maddiewadeauthor.co.uk
Facebook page: https://www.facebook.com/maddieuk/
Facebook group: https://www.facebook.com/groups/546325035557882/
Amazon Author page: amazon.com/author/maddiewade
Goodreads: https://www.goodreads.com/author/show/14854265.Maddie_Wade
Bookbub: https://partners.bookbub.com/authors/3711690/edit
Twitter: @mwadeauthor
Pinterest: @maddie_wade
Instagram: Maddie Author

Printed in Great Britain
by Amazon

86146831R00139